EAD FOR DREAMING

Richard Daniels

Adam,
Thanks for
the
Support
Keep on rockin!

RD

PLASTIC BRAIN PRESS

Plastic Brain Press

Horncastle
Lincolnshire
United Kingdom

plasticbrainpress@gmail.com

www.plasticbrainpress.com

First published in Great Britain in 2018

ISBN-13: 978-1-9998827-2-3

ISBN-10: 1-9998827-2-5

Cover design: Melody Clark

Copyright © 2018 by Richard Daniels

Order of Service

Dedicated to the residents of Low Scaraby

FUCKNUCKLE

This world is sick, this nation is sick, this bathroom is sick, this mirror is sick. You useless piece of goddamn shit. You think your feelings or thoughts add up to anything that isn't shit? You're awake again and during the night those feelings of disgust have not disappeared into the dark – you knew they wouldn't. They are with you in the mirror again. The world has not altered, the smell of your crotch has not altered, the bad news on the radio has not altered; only the words have changed.

Does it feel like you have been running toward this? Pushing through until your feet are thumping on an expanse of sun baked dirt that only stretches further and further into a distance that is painful to gaze at. That's why you stand close to the mirror; fill up the frame, wipe away the steam and stare, trying to see where these thoughts are coming from, like looking for tiny air bubbles from an inner tube in a bucket of water.

Like a drunk in a foreign country you have chased the parade down the late night streets, following the laughter and the singing because you think there's someplace this parade is going to take you. A courtyard of midnight merriments where all the locals will welcome you, push daughters or dark eyed sons at you. What happens?

You fucknuckle.

You turn the corner and the parade has vanished. The merriment has turned to smoke and drifted into the trees of the city – just one more layer of smog and dirt and nothing else but the night patiently waiting for the street cleaners.

You can look into this mirror. You want to conjure that carnival out of the dripping tap and the distant noises of the morning. You even think you could find those back streets where the locals will welcome you, but you won't. You're a piece of shit and so is the world.

SKATEBOARDING WITH JAMES DEAN

My Monday always starts with a 4.30am alarm call. Not from a bedside clock but from a lorry pouring a thousand empty bottles into its rusty stomach. The glass bottles shriek and clatter and cut my eyes open, my brain starts firing. Every Monday. Those shattering cries come from a few streets away where a pub keeps its giant bottle bin, but it feels as if the screams are rising from a cold, lonely darkness that commands me to face the world once more. I fucking hate how Monday begins.

But really I dislike every day just the same. If you go to a job you hate then maybe you understand me on this. My job has trapped me. I started out thinking it was the right thing for me to be doing; going to an office where serious people walk purposefully on carpet tiles that harmonise with the company colours. I thought it was expected of a person. I thought that I too ought to do the kind of job where I wore a tie and strode with purpose for the good of the company, which in return monitored my performance dispassionately and paid just enough so that I would keep doing it. I am angry with my younger self for accepting such a state of affairs. It's no good now though. It is what I do.

Melissa tells me I should not worry so much. She says she used to feel just the same. Melissa lives on the floor below me. We met on the day she moved in to the apartment block – she was struggling up the stairs with a coffee table and I offered to help. We carried pretty much everything she had up the two flights of stairs from the street. All the time she didn't stop talking. Later, when we had become friends, Melissa told me how nervous she had been, how she had split up from her partner after finally realising he was a total twat and decided to get her own place for the first time in her life. She had moved a long way from everything she knew and come to this apartment in a town between two large cities and with a view of bleak hills in the distance. Melissa said she felt comforted by those hills. From her side of the building she could see them from her window and always felt they were keeping an eye on us in a kindly way. To me it felt like those hills had me cornered.

She was about the only other person in the building that I talked to – everybody had that look on their face like they didn't want interactions or else they just looked right through you. I recognised one or two people from where I worked. We always nodded awkwardly. There was also the old maintenance man, Phil. I talked to him but we usually just exchanged pleasantries and joked about how shit things were with the building falling apart and how useless the letting agency was.

Often I would go down to Melissa's flat in the evening. She said she liked to cook and it was better to cook for two people than one. Two or three times a week she invited me down. It was good. We talked a lot. She had her place set out in a way that was very cosy. I teased her about all the cushions and blankets she had thrown over her sofa but really it made the place feel right. I used to sit amongst the cushions and we'd chat while she stood in her kitchenette making dinner. In the winter, bundles of tree branches were cast across her windows by the streetlamps, like shadowy fingers trying to get in. It made it feel even better to be on her sofa, surrounded by cushions and with a glass of red in my hand. It was on such a night that she told me how she beat her feelings of anxiety and doom.

I'd told her about how I felt, about my job and how sometimes I didn't know what to do, like all my possibilities had dwindled to almost nothing at all.

"You need to forget that," she told me. "Change your thinking."

"How?" I demanded.

"For a start you can go skateboarding."

I laughed and drank more wine.

"What I mean to say," she said sitting down with her own glass of Tempranillo, "is *psychic*
skateboarding. If you need to change your mental architecture – and you definitely do – then you should try it. It's what I do."

So Melissa told me about skateboarding with James Dean.

"Who's one of the coolest people to ever walk the Earth? James Dean, that's who. Just think about how at ease he seemed to the world. I don't care how tortured they say he was, James Dean was cool and he knew he was cool. That's a mind-set. That's a place we can go to and our means of transport is the skateboard.

"When I feel like I can't cope with all the shitty things that are in front of me I go skateboarding with James Dean. Me and Jimmy used to go cruising all the time – not so much now because I feel a lot better but I know he's always on hand to go out if ever I need to. I know he'd go boarding with you too."

"I don't get it," I told her. "James Dean died in a car crash. I don't see how he can help me. I'd be better off going back to the doctor and getting on those pills again. They'd make me feel like I was trucking with Bogart."

She winced. "Trucking? No, no, no. That wouldn't be right at all – and not with Bogart. Of course James Dean died. I'm not saying he didn't but that doesn't mean you can't locate him. Psychically. And it doesn't mean you can't go skateboarding with him. Have you ever been on a skateboard before?"

"No. Maybe for about ten minutes when I was twelve years old. I fell off."

"That doesn't matter either. When things get too much you have to grab your board, give Jimmy a call and just go."

I think I must have looked at Melissa like she'd just put a bag of bloody eyeballs on the table and told me to help myself because she laughed at me.

"It's a mind-set remember." She put down her glass. "Close your eyes and ask Jimmy to show you what to do. There he is – maybe it's in bright technicolour or maybe that crisp black and white, but there he is and he's got his skateboard. It's beautiful; a little worn on the deck but still a beautiful thing. When he slaps it down on the tarmac it makes that great clunking sound as the wheels start to roll and his plimsolled feet are on the board and he's looking back and smiling at you while his body is just gliding and carving that board left, then right, cruising along the empty pavement. You're right behind him and you both feel the sunshine on your skin. You both push your feet hard on to the ground and move along with a little more pace. As you go you hit a downslope and the boards pick up speed all by themselves and so you both roll with it and Jimmy Dean is calling back to you about how good this feels and how you've got this under control. He's right. You and Jimmy are gliding along and there's a big orange sun in the sky and you can feel it on you and all around you and those polyurethane wheels are gurgling along. You and James Dean are rolling together. He's whooping at you and you're whooping back at him and all you feel is bliss and in control."

Melissa stopped. I had closed my eyes and I was sat on her sofa with a big grin on my face.

"There, you see," she said slapping my leg. "You're skateboarding with James Dean. You can do it any time you need to. Fuck the rest of the world. It's just you and Jimmy."

I left her place that night thanking her for dinner and telling her she was crazy. She just smiled and said, "If you had one day when you didn't have to be all confused and you didn't feel ashamed of everything."

I shrugged. "That would be something," I told her.

"Try it," she said closing her door and the soft familiar scent of her flat was replaced by the abstract smell of the hallway.

Maybe that night it seemed silly to me but in the darkness of Monday morning at 4am, lying in bed and waiting for the screaming glass to announce the start of another week, skateboarding with James Dean felt right. It felt like it made sense. It took me to a different place where James Dean was grinning at me and whooping as our boards rolled along a boulevard beneath the shadows of palm trees. Cold Britain disappeared. The distant hills evaporated. The glass bottles were silenced.

HEXAGASM

The Gravedigger:

It was December 1979. At the far end of the churchyard was a big old shed where they kept the mower, which was also used for the village green. That's where I slept that night. The vicar told me I could have a room in the rectory but I didn't fancy it – felt like I'd have to be on my best behaviour or something and I preferred my own company; well me and Johnny Walker.

You see there'd been a cold snap and three of Low Scaraby's eldest residents had perished in one night. Old folk don't do well with the cold. Bodies were piling up and with Christmas coming they wanted them buried quick. It was all hands to the pump as they say but I was the only pair of hands actually digging the graves; three of them! The ground being solid didn't help matters.

Anyways, I'd offered to stay over in order to make an early start that next day. I lived in the neighbouring village to Scaraby and didn't want to waste time in the morning. That's when the vicar offered a room and I told him no thank you. The shed had an old stove and I had a fold up bed set with plenty of blankets just next to it. I told the vicar I'd be right as rain and could get started first thing.

There I was with my scotch to keep warm and a good old book about the war. It must've been around midnight when the rattling on the shed door woke me. Next thing I see there was a bloke stood there in front of me holding out a lantern so that I could hardly see his face. He was old though; I thought it must've been snowing as his hair was so white.

I sat up in bed wondering what the bloody hell was going to happen.

"Are you the gravedigger?" this fella asked solemnly. I told him I was. He said his name was Amias Gilbert and he was from the Gravediggers' Union. I'd never heard of such a thing, but he flashed me a card with some sort of insignia on it. I may be a lowly gravedigger but I'm bright enough to know when to keep my mouth shut and listen. There was something about Amias Gilbert I knew was bad and I knew if I didn't pay heed to him I was likely to find out just how bad.

The figure pulled up a stool and sat himself down with the lantern on the floor between us. His cloak was black as the church door hinges and I couldn't tell what were shadow and what were Mr Gilbert. He saw me trembling and told me to have a drink. Well of course I poured a large one and he sat there not taking his eyes from me.

"How'd you know I was here?" I asked him, fearing he had already disturbed the vicar.

He smiled like a snake. "You are a gravedigger," he said. "It is my job to know where you are."

Well that put the wind up me even more so I just nodded.

"You have a grave here by the far wall," he goes on. "It has simple stone but with a geometric carving upon its head; lines that look somewhat like rays of sunlight. This grave belongs to a Mr Gunter Riediger. Do you know such a plot?"

I shook my head. I can't know all the bloody graves and once I've dug them I forget them. "Is something wrong with it?" I asked.

"I want you to exhume Mr Riediger. There is something I need inside his coffin."

Alls I could think to do was have another mouthful of scotch. "I don't know," I told him. "I don't think I'm supposed to. It's illegal or sacrilegious or something."

He leans in closer so that his face is above the lantern. "That is not your concern," he says and with all the shadows on his features I swear I saw the devil behind his eyes.

Next thing I'm heaving away at soil while this Mr Gilbert is perched against another grave smoking a pipe. I keep digging and by god I'm sweating even though there were frost twinkling in the moonlight. An all the time I'm thinking this bloke's nothing but a grave robber but I daren't say anything and I keep expecting the vicar to appear and fly into a terrible rage.

At last I strike the coffin lid and Amias Gilbert gets excited. I prise the lid open. I never seen a corpse before, not like that; dead for two or three years and like some shrunken waxwork in a suit. This Gunter Riediger had his arms crossed upon his chest, clutching hold of something. That were the thing my companion wanted. This terrible look of glee came over his face and gave me the shivers. Gilbert grabbed hold of these two metal canisters that the corpse had in its arms. Now I know they had some old film inside but right then I wasn't sure of a bloody thing, only that I was going to be in serious trouble.

I expected Gilbert to scarper as soon as he got what he wanted but he surprised me. First he gave me a cigarette and then fetched the scotch. He stayed by the graveside and resumed smoking his pipe whilst I filled the hole I'd dug.

Just as I was finishing he stood and said it was time for him to leave. "You have done humanity a great service tonight," he tells me. Then he says, "Do not worry about the ground looking disturbed. The snow will come." With that he took his lantern and his canisters and disappeared. I didn't know what to think of any of it. I was bloody exhausted though, so I went back to the shed and crawled under the blankets.

When I awoke later that morning, bleary and confused, I opened the door to find there was three foot of snow on the ground. I dug no more graves that day and by the time the snow had gone no one was any the wiser about the disturbance at Gunter Riediger's grave.

The Academic:

Good afternoon and welcome to Lindesege University's annual Halloween lecture. My name is Dr Harry Brinkhill and it is my great delight to talk to you today about possibly the greatest filmmaker you've never heard of. If not the greatest then certainly one of the creepiest.

The life and work of Gunter Riediger has been very much forgotten, in no small part because this was the wish of Riediger himself. He only made three films and one of those has been considered a 'lost' work since the 1980s. However, the legends surrounding his films have grown and only gained greater potency since his death in 1977. In recent years a small band of contemporary underground and independent filmmakers have begun to cite him as an influence. So, was Gunter Riediger just another fetishist of gore, psychological trauma and titillation?

Or was he a true visionary with something startling and new to offer us?

My interest in Riediger has been a part of my own film fandom as well as a part of my academic work for several years and much of this evening's lecture is taken from my critique of the director due to be published by McGuffin Press later next month.

Who then, was Gunter Riediger? In many ways he is an enigma: a failure, a pioneer, an outsider. He resists interpretation. However, that is what we must attempt tonight if we wish to understand what a genius he might have been and in so doing try to conjure his spirit on this Halloween night.

Riediger was born in Lubeck in Germany in 1916 but moved to Berlin when he was three years old after the death of his father in the Kaiserschlacht offensive of 1918. By all accounts he was a quiet, insular boy who seemed happiest when he was playing alone, free to let his imagination take him to new worlds. School friends remember him being fascinated by legends of knights and chivalry from Germany's distant past. In early 1930s Berlin, when Riediger came of age, he found his interest with legends of past glory was also shared by his step-father along with the leaders of the growing National Socialist Party. Details of just how deeply Riediger believed in what became Hitler's Third Reich are uncertain at best and this lecture is not the place to go into it with any detail. Simply put, my research suggests, and my impressions are, that Gunter Riediger was a spiritual person with a powerful imagination. There is little evidence to support that he was a fervent Nazi as some have claimed. Rather, it is more likely he was a young man unavoidably swept along in the tide of a nation's mass derangement. We know for certain that he left Germany at the earliest opportunity.

Also, what is certain is that growing up in inter-war Berlin gave him direct access to German Expressionism as well as everything else that was on offer in the culturally innovative city. We know his film career began when he worked as one of many assistants in the making of Riefenstahl's *Triumph of the Will.*

Riediger fled his homeland in 1939; first to England and then to the New World, specifically Hollywood, California. He worked for one of the smaller studios, Gower Pictures, which produced a slew of films from the 30s through to the late 50s in genres such as westerns, detective, comedy and adventure. This was certainly where Riediger learnt his trade in the movie business.

It wasn't until 1967 that Riediger made his own full directorial debut for the big screen. He was fifty one years old. *Zombie Bikers From Beach Town* may have been considered a B-movie horror, yet it is significant for featuring Terence Hickey in the hero role, doing battle against the titular bikers. Hickey was an African-American actor. Many consider George A. Romero's *Night of the Living Dead* to be the first time a black actor was given the role of a hero, however Riediger's debut did it twelve months earlier. *Zombie*

Bikers also featured elements of documentary filmmaking, fake news clips and intensely expressionistic use of photography; all things which have become commonplace today.

Riediger's next film, *Sagiquarius,* was a full colour, countercultural, psychedelic journey that rivalled Roger Corman's *The Trip* and *Head* by The Monkees. Once again it had little commercial impact at the time and went fairly unnoticed by the film going public in any demographic other than deadheads.

Finally then, comes *Hexagasm*, Riediger's lost masterpiece. Made in 1973, Riediger had spent the previous three years travelling with his new wife whom he had met whilst filming *Sagiquarius.* Vivian Arnold, known professionally as Vivian LeVega, was a young British actress and by all accounts what she lacked in talent she made up in smouldering, mysterious beauty. Together they spent nearly two years travelling through South America. Riediger never spoke about his experiences of their expedition, though it is speculated he became a convert to a mystical indigenous brand of tribal voodoo involving the ingestion of Ayahausca. In any event he returned from the jungle with a script: *Hexagasm.*

So what is *Hexagasm*? What is the film about? This is an incredibly difficult question to answer. It involves necromancy, schizophrenia, nudity, explosions, blood, guts and paganism. Today only brief clips of it survive but those who have seen the footage are convinced that the whole was something incredibly powerful. Film critic Stanley Dean has remarked, 'Not unlike Brian Wilson's once lost musical masterpiece *Smile*, the film *Hexagasm* has rightly begun to develop its own underground legend. From its surviving fragments one can only imagine the whole and rue that it has been lost. Perhaps some things are too evolutionary as well as revolutionary. Some things people will not understand for a long time. I believe *Hexagasm* is such a film.'

Riediger himself is the force behind the film's disappearance. Orcus Films had arranged a private premiere where many of the cast and crew, as well as several critics, were flown to a location just outside of San Francisco for the first ever screening. The film had been well received by all, however tragedy struck on the return journey. The chartered aircraft got into difficulties and crashed in the wilderness of Big Sur. Many involved in the film were killed. In the following months others involved with *Hexagasm* and Orcus Films suffered tragic accidents. It wasn't long before people started talking about a curse. Before any significant release could happen Riediger made the decision to pull the plug. He bought the film back from the studio, including the master tapes. A short time later he moved with Vivian to the UK and refused to ever speak of his film again.

Gunter Riediger only lived for another two years himself, suffering a massive heart attack in 1977. He is buried in the village church yard of Low Scaraby where he had retired to with Vivian. She too passed away six months later; unable to cope alone she took her own life.

Stories of the film's curse as well as its greatness never went away. Legend has it that Riediger went as far as having the tape reels buried with him to prevent the film ever being shown in its entirety. Even today there are rumours that the tapes were grave robbed some years after his death and are now out in the world somewhere only waiting to be rediscovered.

Next I would like to…*

**Dr Brinkhill was killed in a hit and run incident in Lincoln just twenty three hours before the annual event at Lindesege University. This was the only file relating to the Halloween Lecture that could be found amongst Dr Brinkhill's work and private computer.*

The Magician:

Where does one begin with something so ancient that it is like the rainbows trapped in oil, hidden until water and light reveal them? How does one make people see colours in the blackness? One must cast a spell that is how.

Imagine you are in the jungle. You are lost. It is vast, and you have been lost for so long that you have forgotten what it is like to not be lost. You have forgotten what it is to not be in the jungle. These things have become invisible to your mind and so you go on each day, hacking through the undergrowth with only the vaguest inclination that one day the jungle will end. You have the suspicion that when that day comes it will be a momentous event.

One day you stumble upon a medicine man. He says he has a gift for you. This shaman knows where the jungle ends, and he can take you there. Don't you want to leave the jungle? Will you follow the shaman and take his medicine?

Allow me to introduce myself. I am a magician, a shaman, a medicine man. My name is Amias Gilbert. I am showing you my hand so that you can see I am hiding nothing. My sleeve is empty too. I can see in your eyes that you are not someone that can be duped. Your brain is much too fierce for that. I can also see a fire in your eyes. You desire to understand, don't you?

For a very long time I have tried to communicate to people the way out of the infinite forest. I am from an ancient tribe of people who have wandered the Earth for more time than you can dream of; through deserts and tundra and through the fields and then through giant cities. Our creed is simple – to free you from the darkness. We hack at the vines that tether you. On an individual level, we have had some success. Minds have been liberated but, more often than not, our singular converts have gone on to experience suffering at the hands of the herd which remain, still crawling in the dirt of the forest floor.

On several occasions in the past we have tried to liberate minds on a mass scale. This has only ended in calamity. Russia 1917. Germany 1933. However, out of these disasters we have learnt much and improved our methods; after all, every magician, even real ones, must employ smoke and mirrors in order to arouse an audience. In Gunter Riediger we had found someone we could adopt and nurture.

From a distance we followed and observed him, first as he fled Europe and then as he developed his career in California. We had already begun to see the power of cinema and the influence it might have. With our magic in combination with his magic we could do such powerful work. It is somewhat ironic that it was his travels through the real jungle of South America that allowed us to introduce ourselves and our ideas to him most fully, so that the jungle of his mind could be cleared. Where most men see myth, Riediger saw truth and understood what power his films might have.

Hexagasm was born.

Very soon we learned there was a problem. Something had gone wrong. Like any medicine the ingredients were many and varied and something designed to cure can quite easily have the opposite effect. Hexagasm was unique and powerful in a way that even we did not understand. The film unleashed something which was never intended to be unleashed. Those who saw it were cursed. Riediger did what he thought was right – he took it away from the world and took himself away too.

However, the world moves on and I move with it. Once again this is a dark time. More than ever people need release from their mind forged forests. I am the shaman. I have the medicine that will set you free. Hexagasm is reborn, re-duxed. From the master tapes a new version has been returned to the world and this time fully effective. One need only watch Riediger's masterpiece and you shall be set free. The truth of existence will open for you. Truly effective mass cleansing is at hand, thanks to the digital world that now exists. At last the time is right.

You no longer need to feel lost. Your journey is at an end. Hexagasm will set you free. You have come this far. I only ask you to take one step further…

For details on how to access the film, contact plasticbrainpress@gmail.com with the keyword 'Hexagasm'

BUGSHOT

Along the limestone track bordered by wild garlic and explosions of ragwort, amid nettles and grass, Ian loved to feel sweat falling from his temples and on to his T-shirt. It told him he was burning energy. His trainers, specifically designed for runners, pounded the rhythm of thud then crackle as his legs propelled him like oar strokes – at least when his body felt good and everything was flowing.

He'd started running more frequently – sometimes four evenings a week – since his girlfriend announced she was pregnant. He'd gotten home from the factory one evening and found Alison in the kitchen. She stood grinning at him while the electric fan, perched on the fridge-freezer, made the multi-coloured streamers above the backdoor ripple like a rainbow peeling apart.

"I'm pregnant," she told him and the fan moved, blowing in Ian's face.

Of course, he was happy. They had planned to get married anyway but now everything became far more intense. Alison wanted to get married sooner, before baby's arrival. She and her mother had switched into overdrive. Ian went running.

He was on the track where the hedgerows waned and fields became visible. They were full of wheat almost ready for harvest. Over his other shoulder was a field which halted abruptly where the town's industrial park rose from behind the wheat tassels. The industrial zone's corrugated warehouses and storage tanks, like tumours, bulged against the sky watching him struggle and sweat as he ran. They disappeared behind trees by the time he got to the overpass. That was where he turned around. His route was not a circuit, only a line repeated. He went out. He came back. The industrial buildings watched his return.

Several years before, when he and Alison started dating, the industrial park was one of the spots they would go to have sex in the back of his car. They were both still living at home with their parents so private time was limited whilst their desires were not. Usually after a late showing at the cinema they would drive to a particular spot. There was one of those roads you get on industrial parks that had been constructed but didn't go anywhere. It ended in concrete barriers overtaken by weeds. There was nothing around but scrub land and a silent engineering workshop. Ian had loved the darkness of the backseats, the awkwardness, the closeness and the emptiness just outside the car's windows.

He got to the underpass where he allowed himself a moment to walk and breathe. He always checked his time at the underpass – it was the furthest outward point. He walked then turned and began retracing the line he had just carved in kinetic energy.

When he ran his thoughts would drift. It was often to Alison and their impending situation but just as he was getting tired, beginning to struggle with the effort of running, that was when his mind would loosen. Sometimes Ian thought it was the true reason he went running – so that he would get to the point where his anxieties weren't able to keep up. That was what he was trying to achieve.

There was something he hadn't told Alison. One big thing that had affected his life more than anything else, yet he found it difficult to speak of, which was why he hadn't mentioned it to her, though he had wanted to. Now they were getting married. Now they were having a baby. Ian felt that if he didn't say something it wouldn't be fair on Alison. They were committing to each other so he ought to tell her about what happened when he was a boy. The guilt he felt. Its memory tingled once more along his sweaty back. Ian pushed his legs harder.

It happened at the industrial estate when he was ten. Years later with Alison, in his car, he desperately tried to fuck away his bad memories of that location. He thought he had succeeded as his efforts gave rise to a genuine and deep love between him and Alison. Ian would sit back on the itchy upholstery of his car seat, holding Alison as they both panted from their lovemaking, and wonder if the bad memories had managed to spawn seeds that had grown into something good. He wondered if he deserved it.

As a boy he often used to play in and around the waste land of the industrial estate – it was close to the playing fields but offered more excitement and adventure. Sometimes he went with the boy from across the street, Thomas Toynton. Thomas wasn't right in the head. At school most children called him a spaka. If they let him hang out with them it was so they could pick on him. Thomas knew this routine and never seemed to mind at the beginning, until someone would take it too far and he would become upset and throw a tantrum. On this afternoon Ian let Thomas tag along with him. Round the back of a warehouse they found a bonfire that was burning low. Ian suggested they try and get it going again and began looking for bits of cardboard that could be thrown on to the embers. Both boys enjoyed the challenge of finding the card as well as throwing it on to the fire and poking it with sticks. After a while they had managed to bring the flames back to life. Ian discovered a trolley that had been dumped. It was full of various household products still in their sealed packages. "This stuff will really burn," he told Thomas and Thomas clapped and agreed.

They began tearing things out of their plastic wombs, lobbing a can of deodorant or air freshener into the fire, then legging it behind a screen of rubble. The cans popped and fizzed in the heat and for an instant the flames would shoot higher. Ian saw an unopened pack of six full cans of insecticide. In stark red and black labels it read BugShot: *Kills anything that flies or crawls!* Ian looked closer and saw the words 'highly flammable' written at the bottom. The cans were big and clearly filled with something malignant.

"I dare you to throw the whole lot into the fire," Ian said turning to Thomas. "If you do you're not a spaka," he added.

Thomas seemed to think about it. Instinct told him this was where the teasing and kicking began. He looked down at the cans of BugShot.

"It will be really cool," Ian told him. "I can tell everyone at school you did it."

"Tell them I'm not a spaka," Thomas said before the grin returned to his face and he was picking up the pack of insecticide.

Ian watched him lumber toward the fire and throw the cans into the middle of it so that ash and sparks were sent into the air. This time Thomas didn't scamper back to the rubble where Ian stood. Instead he waited, wanting to see the cans and their plastic begin to bubble and burn. They did. The air changed rapidly. Ian could smell the chemical fug from his position twenty feet away. Then there was the detonation, the cans shearing as their content became unstable and mutated into something more deadly, more aggressive. There was no explosion but a dull metallic *thunk,* like a hammer against an anvil. Noxious vapour and metal shards flew out from the fire as if a party popper filled with nails and glass had been pulled. Thomas let out a terrible shrieking cry and fell to the floor. He rolled on the uneven ground and wouldn't stop screaming. Ian didn't know what to do. He couldn't move. He stood there, inert, like the rubble.

Ian felt a drop of sweat fall from the bridge of his nose, his tongue catching it and enjoying the salty tang. He pumped his arms harder and wondered if his soon to be mother in law would still be at home when he returned.

Up ahead something appeared from the hedgerow. It seemed to move then came to a stop in the middle of the track. Ian thought it might have been an animal but as he got closer he realised it wasn't. He stopped running as soon as he saw what it was. Laid on its side was a dented and old looking can of BugShot. Ian drew up and walked slowly toward it, his body feeling the sudden lack of movement, making his skin buzz. He looked down at the battered can. BugShot: *Kills anything that flies or crawls!* It looked old – they hadn't made the stuff for years – but seeing a can of it again made the afternoon with Thomas by the bonfire come back. That afternoon was always in the shadows but now it was right in front of him, on the track he ran when he wanted to sweat and tire himself so that he would sleep. He had seen the can from a distance and thought it a creature. It seemed to come from the undergrowth but now Ian wasn't so sure. Had it just rolled unbidden out from under the long grass and come to a stop in the middle of the track? He glanced about but there was no one around, not even a dog walker, only a wood pigeon flying clumsily over the field.

Ian stared at the can lying on its side. Thomas Toynton had been rushed to hospital but died from his injuries the following morning. Ian knew he had done something terrible though most were sympathetic and told him he shouldn't blame himself, Thomas Toynton was just that kind of kid. He did things for attention and look what happened. Ian knew differently.

He crouched and looked more closely at the insecticide and its worn red and black label. He noticed a slight charring at its base. Sweat now covered him. A bead of it fell from his chin and on to the can. He picked the can up. He could feel there was some liquid inside when he shook it. The can began to make a weak whistle, like something escaping. Ian remembered the sickening, sulphuric odour. The whistle changed. Became louder. Thomas Toynton was screaming again as the fragments of steel and plastic tore into the skin of his face and arms.

Ian dropped the can back on to the track. It made a dull clank and rolled a little before exploding. He felt the sudden swell of heat from the bonfire and the savage pain that enveloped him in only a moment. It surrounded him like a cloud that was thick and caustic and filled with anguish. Ian fell down on to the scrub and was gone.

The track was deserted with not even a dog walker. Only a delicate breeze whisked over the hedgerow making the nettles loll, forcing butterflies from their brief pause.

TRASH CAN MANIFESTO

Dear whoever you are,

If you are reading this then you must have taken it from whichever filth ridden receptacle I have left it in. I congratulate you on your curiosity and sincerely hope that you do not make a living by eradicating or collecting the redundant and used ephemera of your world. If you do, then we can be considered comrades in arms and this is my petition to you.

I am a FAIRY.

I say this proudly.

As a mortal human you cannot comprehend what the true life of a fairy is, however it is my desperate hope that this letter will help you understand my world and my reasons for writing what you hold in your hands.

As fairies we are indoctrinated to be ignorant. Ignorant to the fact that our lives are full of limitation and so much is already predetermined even before we get our wings. The elders would have us believe that all fairies are equal and all have the same potential. I'm sad to say this is a lie.

There are many class of fairies. I am sure you are aware of this. There are tooth fairies, flower fairies, fairies of the forest, garden and river. There is even the Angel of Death; he is not really an angel, just a big, mean, shithouse, fucker of a fairy. Truth be told I like him. He's funny. So you can see; there are fairies you've heard of but then there are the fairies you haven't.

For instance, there are photocopier fairies who dwell amongst the innards of photocopying machines. They collect, bag and ship dust and ink powder back to Moonsfield. This is the land where all fairies come from. More than likely you know it by the name of Fairyland or some such nonsense.

There are sofa fairies who collect, bag and ship fluff and crumbs from the back of your sofas straight to Moonsfield.

Flower fairies that collect, bag and ship pollen. Grease fairies for oil and grime. Coffee fairies for grounds, they also deal with tea leaves. All these fairies exist.

Humans and fairies have, in many ways, evolved side by side. Think of us as the white blood cells of humanity. Your world feeds ours and our world thrives by cleaning and maintaining yours.

These are not the only fairies. There are also those that never even enter your world – they are the ones whose job it is to stay in Moonsfield to create and administrate our world from all that we collect from you. Our world built on the detritus of yours. A nice, happy symbiotic relationship, right?

Well I say no. No more.

Moonsfield is a world of oppressive control, where big fairy is always watching us, where once given our roles there is little or no opportunity for change. No chance to express yourself in another way, no other occupation for you, no questioning, no social mobility, no space in which to declare: 'I could be…'

Sure, there is a certain security – your place in Moonsfield, your brothers, sisters and comrades. There is the narcotic escape of fairy dust which you can snort in glittering lines from here to Oberon's palace. It is even tacitly encouraged. You are free to be content but not free to choose. Not free to be dissatisfied. Not free to say no, this is wrong.

Why should you care about any of this? I do not know. You, in your world of liberation, where you are free to become whoever you want to be without hierarchies and systems of control handed down to you by elites. Where you are not encouraged to sedate yourself on mindless distractions or silly entertainments. How I want to scream when we fairies gather for frolicking and to gorge ourselves on the projection of moonbeams, dancing across the walls of every dwelling in Moonsfield. 'This is wrong,' I want to shout. 'Can you not see? We could have so much more.'

Let me be clear; I am desperate. I can no longer act as if all is well and so these words, this letter, is an act of the utmost rebellion. The fairies will judge me as a traitor. We are not supposed to make our existence known to humankind. That is our golden rule. My act of defiance will mean I am excommunicated but it is something that I have thought long and hard about. I am prepared to make this sacrifice in order to reveal the truth and change things. That is, as I understand, the power of words, the power of creativity. Therefore, I defy Moonsfield and all its structures.

If you value what you have in your world then pity me. I have given you knowledge of the fairies and now I ask that you seek them out in all the places where the detritus of your world collects. The knowledge I have imparted to you will rock the very foundations of Oberon's grand palace and all fairies below it.

I can no longer live the life that has been handed to me. What is that life you will ask? Which type of fairy am I? I am one of those sprites that you will not have heard of; not cherished like tooth fairies, not idealised like flower fairies. I am a used tissue fairy. I dwell among the waste bins and laundry baskets, harvesting the snot rags you have discarded as nothing but a snare for your tears and ectoplasmic secretions. Every day I scavenge then transport used tissues from your world to mine where their contents is turned into the walls and pavements of Moonsfield itself. My task is invisible to you but believe me, it is almost invisible to the fairies as well – even though the fruit of my labour is everywhere they go.

This letter is my cry for freedom. If you cherish and value the freedoms that you have then I urge you to hear these words and seek out what is invisible, what is extraordinary, that exists amongst you every day.

Yours with hope

Fafner Krustfluffle.

THE CULPEPER PROJECT

Lincolnshire, 1965

The young man pressed his back against the stonework a little more and looked upward at the arch of the flying buttress. Like a bat wing it grew from the cathedral wall, flinging outward then down dramatically into the manicured lawn. Henry Ingram removed his glasses and gave them another wipe. Beneath the buttress arch he had managed to keep dry but the mizzle had gradually begun to close about him.

It was not how he had wanted his first assignment to begin. After graduating from Cambridge he'd hoped some dynamic existence of clandestine adventure awaited him. He had idly imagined arriving somewhere like Paris, pulling into the Gard Du Nord at midnight, or even sweeping into New York with a cheery American associate saying 'welcome to the United States Mr Ingram.' He had not daydreamed about catching his death in an isolated county town like Lincoln. A large drop of rain slipped past the collar of his overcoat like an icy finger down his back. Henry cursed as a shiver ran through him.

In the gloomily silent morning he heard the noise of an engine getting closer until a black Zephyr was pulling up at the side of the road a little way in front of him. Henry scurried across the lawn, leaving the shelter of the cathedral stone. The driver had already wound down the passenger window by the time he reached the car. Suddenly self-conscious Henry bent his head toward the opening.

"What's your name?" the middle-aged man behind the wheel asked.

Henry thought for a second. “Hellebore,” he told him. “Black Hellebore.” He glanced about but there was no one to observe their exchange. The world was still asleep beneath a large grey blanket.

The driver jabbed a thumb at himself. “Mandrake.”

“Yes.”

“Well get in then. You’re letting the warmth out.”

The car drove on even before Henry had shut the door.”

The man at the wheel looked around fifty years of age; his hair was almost entirely grey and cut in the ex-military style, as was the neat moustache sitting squarely above his top lip. He did not look at Henry. Eyes that suggested an inflexible power of concentration looked out at the road ahead. The ancient stone cottages of the cathedral quarter had been replaced by post-war housing. They were leaving Lincoln.

"First assignment isn't it?" Mandrake asked, his tone as neutral as the wiper blades stroking across the windscreen.

"Yes, it is." Henry hoped he sounded diligent. "Is there anything I should know?"

An eye, blue like a police box, turned on him for an instant. "You read the file?"

"Of course." Being out in the drizzle suddenly didn't seem quite so bad. Henry now felt a rigidity in his muscles that had been shivering just moments before. Everything seemed real suddenly. The Zephyr's interior had the fragrance of stale cigar smoke and Brylcreem, suffocating his expectations of adventure even more.

"But?" Mandrake accelerated and changed gears.

"Well," Henry looked out at the landscape of soggy green fields. "I must say I didn't entirely grasp what it was all about. I don't think I've been provided clearance for some of the code words." He wished he'd given the file more thorough attention but it had been late and he'd gotten the feeling it was nothing more than some sort of low level data handling project.

"Indeed?" Mandrake sucked his teeth. "To which code words are you referring?"

Henry was uncertain if this were a test. "Magician and Oracle. I couldn't fathom what they were ciphers for. I found the whole file to be somewhat, well, vague, I suppose."

"When did you arrive in Lincoln?"

"Last night sir."

"Mandrake will do." Henry wondered if it was annoyance in his superior's voice or just a natural condescension to new recruits. "What you find unclear, Hellebore, will become less so, though in its turn, what becomes clearer only renders other things more tenebrous. For today I would advise you to go with the flow, as your generation so frequently does."

"Yes Mandrake."

"The Magician," Mandrake went on, "Is a gentleman by the name of Enoch Kessel." He smiled faintly. "Enoch does not have full clearance within the Culpeper Project and he is not part of the service. We have brought him in due to his unique knowledge. He helped develop radar systems during the war."

"Does the Magician know we are coming?"

"Just keep your mouth shut and observe," Mandrake advised. "You might even learn enough to enjoy a second assignment."

They drove into the village of Low Scaraby. At its crossroads they turned right. Henry thought it looked a pleasant enough place, it was only the mizzle which made it seem forsaken. Once past the edge of a small wood, Mandrake turned the car on to a narrow farm road leading to a house that sat amongst fields empty but for lapwings poking the soil.

A man was at the door of the house even before Mandrake had switched the engine off. His hair was white and uncombed and his thin face had at least two days of stubble on it.

"It's working Mr Mandrake. I tell you, it has come to life!"

"This is Enoch," Mandrake told Henry in a low voice as they got out of the Zephyr.

Enoch glanced nervously back inside the house. "The first signal came through at about 3am. I've been able to refine it and about an hour ago…well," he appeared to run out of words and put a hand through his hair.

"Calm yourself Enoch," Mandrake smiled. "We have a new associate with us today. This is Black Hellebore."

Henry nodded while Enoch only seemed to stare through him. "Yes," Enoch said absently. "Black Hellebore." The old man turned back to Mandrake.

"You must see. This is the breakthrough we've wanted."

"Then let us go inside. You can make us all some tea and then we shall see what is what."

Henry followed Mandrake's lead. He said nothing and began urgently trying to recall everything he had read in the file the night before. It was an espionage project, he knew that. It was something intended to listen to the Soviets and used classified technology. The latest information in the file suggested the project had stalled and was due to be shut down.

All three men went into the house. Enoch brought them to his kitchen where there was a large table. Henry observed how messy the place was but, he thought, at least there was a hearth and it was warm. On the table there were strange bits of electronic parts, none of which Henry could identify. At the centre was a metallic box about the size of a briefcase. It had several blinking lights and a small oscilloscope, like the eye of a cyclops, which seemed to watch them as they sat down. Henry could see no source of power for the machine and guessed it somehow worked from a battery.

"It has certainly developed since last I was here," said Mandrake looking at the box.

"The spirits have made contact," Enoch told him. "It finally works."

Henry looked at his superior. Mandrake only responded with a flinty gaze. "You must calm yourself Enoch. All good science requires proof, as you know."

"We are beyond science," Enoch shook his head. "I tell you this is a greater power than we can understand. That I can prove."

"And that is why we are here. We hope to understand the secrets of the eastern bloc. Do not forget our purpose."

"Him," Enoch pointed a shaking finger at Henry. "He has come from Cambridge. Henry is his name. His father died in the war. I'm right aren't I?"

"How do you know this?" Henry demanded. He looked again at Mandrake who appeared surprised but unconcerned. "Who's leaked this information?" Henry asked again.

"The Oracle," Enoch told him. "The spirits have spoken through it, I tell you."

"I'm afraid our superiors will require a little more than that," Mandrake said calmly. "While sensitive, that information is hardly unattainable. It only suggests the sloppiness of our colleagues in London."

"It's bloody cheeky," Henry protested. "Surely this project has been compromised if that kind of information has leaked."

"Quiet, Hellebore," Mandrake told him, and turned to the Magician. "Is that all there is Enoch?"

"I will show you. Then you will see."

Enoch flipped a switch on the side of the machine. It crackled. The oscilloscope glowed green and began to quiver. He fiddled with a dial on the side. A static noise grew from a speaker at its rear, the frequency constantly shifting.

"This is ridiculous," Henry muttered.

"Quiet," Mandrake told him again.

The static suddenly seemed to settle, clicking and buzzing with a regular pulse. Henry could feel the hair standing up on the back of his neck and for the second time that morning a shiver ran down his spine.

"It's found something," Enoch whispered. "The spirits have returned."

Mandrake ran a finger across his moustache, expectantly. "Go on then Enoch. Here is your opportunity."

Enoch nodded. "Spirits!" he cried. "Are you there? Can you communicate through this machine?"

The metallic box continued to buzz.

"Spirits!" Enoch began again.

Before he could say more the static began to quiver, its pitch higher. Out of the fuzz a voice came through, something human and also machine-like too.

"I am here Mr Kessel," said the voice. "There are others with you now. Strangers."

"These are my friends," Enoch informed the machine.

The oscilloscope wavered in silence for a moment. The voice replied. "You do not have friends Mr Kessel."

"We have many things to ask you," Enoch went on.

"Does this spirit have a name?" Henry whispered.

"His name is Mr Sawyer," Enoch told him. "He came through last night. That is when he told me about you, to expect this visit."

Henry's guts told him to get away from the place and he would have if it were his decision. He looked at Mandrake. The commanding officer had an intrigued expression.

"Ask it if it knows anything of the Soviet operations in Murmansk and the Barents Sea," Mandrake told Enoch.

Enoch obeyed.

"That is of no concern to me," came the reply from Mr Sawyer in his synthetic voice. "I will tell you this however; one of you does not have long left in the mortal realm. I sense they will not see tomorrow."

"I am sorry Mr Mandrake," Enoch said turning one of the dials. "But I am sure with more work and fine tuning we can obtain valuable information."

"Did you hear what it said?" Henry asked, his body seeming to feel the cold again.

Mandrake waved his concerns away. "A great deal of time and effort has already been spent on this project, Enoch. I, nor my superiors, are convinced it will provide the meaningful results as we had hoped for."

"We are communicating with the dead!" Enoch looked from Mandrake to Henry. "I have created this machine with great toil and difficulty," he said more desperately.

"And with our funding," Mandrake reminded him.

"We are on the brink of being able to answer so many of life's questions. At the final step you wish to turn away?"

"Questions of life are not the kind my superiors want answers to."

Enoch's machine began to crackle once more, as if the station had been lost. The oscilloscope wavered frantically as the static grew louder. In an instant the noise stopped and was replaced by a high pitched whistle. Henry cupped his hands over his ears. All three men pulled away from the table where the machine was beginning to shake.

"Your living world is nothing but a puppet show." Mr Sawyer spoke again but his voice deeper, more infected by the electronic fog. Henry sensed a darkness in the voice, a vibration to the tone that had no benevolence. It made him feel a despair within. "When the strings are cut," the voice continued, "you will fall and know the void. The void through which you can do nothing else but fall."

"That is enough," Mandrake decreed. "Turn it off."

The bare electric light above their heads flickered and the entire room began to rattle as if a wind were sweeping through the chimney and out through the hearth.

"You who speaks with authority," barked Mr Sawyer. "I see your soul. Your existence is so empty that all you ever do is try and outrun its emptiness. Your wife knows this and despises you, yet she is all you have. She no longer comforts you when you wake, screaming at all the terrible things you have seen. Screaming at the terrible things you did in the war."

"Turn it off," Mandrake demanded.

"Your wife reaches out to other lovers in the times you are away. She is unhappy when you return. Inside you know this, Mandrake, and yet you hide it from yourself and make both your lives miserable."

The door of the stove flung itself open and a cloud of ash and dust blew from it. Henry felt sure he saw the cloud form into a demonic figure with arms reaching out toward Mandrake as if to scoop him up. There was another shrieking burst of noise from the machine and the demon dissipated into smoke, filling the room with ash.

"Enough!" Mandrake shouted, grabbing the box and throwing it to the floor. "This project is terminated."

Enoch fell to his knees to protect his machine but Mandrake kicked him away, grabbing hold of the oracle, its blinking lights and oscilloscope now dark.

"I will recommend that this project is to be shut down and its funding withdrawn. Your time here, Enoch, has come to an end. British Intelligence has indulged your clairvoyant claptrap long enough. Smash this place to bits," Mandrake told Henry. "I'll be in the car." He marched out clutching the machine.

Henry looked at Enoch, whimpering on the floor. The air smelt of cold soot.

"The dead know things," Enoch told him in a whisper. "They know our frailties."

Henry grabbed the old man and sat him in a chair. He looked at his worn face. He had been trained to read faces but now didn't understand what he saw. "I am sorry," he told him, and left.

He got back in the Zephyr and Mandrake dumped the metal box on his lap. He felt a residual warmth from its casing.

“Let me remind you,” Mandrake told him as they sped away from the farmhouse, “that what you have seen this morning is classified. You have no clearance to speak about it and you will not be writing any report. Is that understood?”

Henry nodded.

The Zephyr bounced along the farm track and back on to the main road toward the village of Low Scaraby. Henry had to hold the oracle tightly. Even though its lights were dead he felt a sense of terrible sorrow seeping into him through his fingers.

“Do you believe it?” he asked Mandrake. “Were we communicating with the dead?”

Mandrake’s hands were claws on the steering wheel. “Enoch Kessel is a sick man. It was a mistake to use him in such a way.” The older man turned to Henry.

"You shall not speak of this or your career will be over before it has begun."

The oracle began to tremble in Henry's hands. Its bulbs remained dark but the thing began to buzz and click like it was searching for a radio station. The trembling became more violent.

"What are you doing?" Mandrake demanded.

"It's the machine!" Henry tried to release his hands from it but couldn't.

Mandrake looked at him. In his eyes Henry saw a look of despair, the kind that came from a fusion of fear and remorse.

There was a loud thud that seemed to silence the oracle. Henry recognised it as the sound of a tyre blowout. It sent the car swerving violently in the opposite lane. He glanced across to his superior but Mandrake seemed frozen, unable to stop the car from leaving the road and nose diving into a dyke. "Damn it all," he muttered. They flipped over and tangled into the fence that marked the boundary of Scaraby Woods.

The car came to rest on its wheels, the engine hissing angrily. Henry still clutched the oracle. A spot of blood appeared on its silver casing from where it was dripping from his broken nose. He looked over and could tell Mandrake was dead by the way his head hung down at an unnatural angle, like his neck was made of paper. His eyes, still with the same wretched demeanour, were open and gazed at the oracle.

A moment later the dented car door groaned as it was pulled open. Enoch Kessel stood panting and looked inside. He didn't say anything, only reaching in to take the machine from Henry's grasp. Henry tried to move but felt a terrible pain shoot through his legs and up his spine.

"The villagers will come for you. They will help," Enoch told him. "I am sorry." Enoch took the oracle and held it tightly to his chest. "I cannot stay." He turned and ran into the darkness of the woods.

ATLANTIS FOR ALL

Themistius looked at the rain striking the window. It had started abruptly and began to fall heavily enough that the grey film of dust on the glass was being washed away. Grey – just the same colour as the mountains in the distance. Mountains that had recently been blasted and carved and shaped and changed forever.

He noticed both troopers and agents outside, getting wet while watching everything going on around them, the people and the vehicles. Of course each vehicle was being scanned as a matter of protocol. The recent events back in the capital were new and deadly and Themistius wondered if there even was a protocol for any of it. Atlantis had never faced something like this before. Just like all the other agents he maintained a look of seriousness; as a high-ranking security advisor he had to maintain the appearance of control more than anyone.

At the edge of the parking lot, through the rain, he could make out the blurred shape of the Emperor's hover jet. It looked awkward with its weight sat on the ground. Even with the weather deteriorating a crowd was gathering, grinning with what Themistius guessed would be excitement in the hope of catching a glimpse of their ruler; Veles. First Lord of Atlantis. The crowd were ignorant to the fact that had the Emperor not left the capital the night before, in order to attend the unveiling of the monument carved into the mountainside, then he would certainly have been killed in the terrorist bomb. It was partly Themistius' job to keep the people ignorant of this.

Inside the café there was an atmosphere of stern assiduity. Agents monitored things on screens from the red padded booths, while data links were made with the capital. The official line being broadcast was that a warehouse fire had caused an explosion which had injured a handful of workers.

The visit by Veles to the mountain monument had been planned months before and the café had always been the intended base for proceedings. Now, with the terrorist attack back in the capital it was more a temporary crisis management station. Two bodyguards stood directly in front of the booth where Themistius was sat opposite the Emperor. It was the morning after the bomb explosion and Themistius had been summoned.

His attention shifted from the window back to the Emperor. Veles appeared to be unflustered by the attempt on his life. Another spoonful of ice cream went through the flexible mouth slot of Veles' prosthetic mask. "How's your tea?" the Emperor asked.

The question startled Themistius and made him look down at his untouched cup.

"You should drink it. You don't look too well." Veles' blank mask nodded at the steaming tea.

"I'm fine sir."

"How many suspects have you rounded up from last night?" Veles got down to business.

"None- yet. After the chaos and confusion following the blast, many of our men were injured. Some killed. It has been a difficult twelve hours."

Veles shook his head. "If the Kosmics get their way this is only a beginning. As I have already said, they should not be underestimated."

"What remains of the scene is still being analysed," Themistius went on. "We have specialists arriving now." He assessed his own performance. He thought it convincing. In all honesty he had no idea if the blackened, crispy remains of what had been the downtown would or could offer any answers.

"How have you been feeling?" Veles squeezed another dollop of ice cream through his mask, his attention fixed on his security advisor.

Themistius wished he hadn't forgotten his sunglasses. What were his eyes giving away to the man in front of him? Could Veles really see what was churning through his heart – or even his mind – just as everybody said? The blank mask looked at him. Themistius suddenly registered that Veles was not wearing his customary white gloves. He could not remember seeing his leader without them. The Emperor's hands revealed a covering of deep red scars where the skin had once been sliced or burnt or both. They had healed but the scar tissue was profound – as if the skin of his hands had been pulled off, turned inside out, then put back. Themistius glanced down at the small cut on the palm of his own hand.

"I noticed your cut," Veles said with a smile in his voice. "Not quite as bad as mine." He drummed his fingers on the table top. "Tell me Themistius, have you been feeling different in any way since your encounter with the mysterious Mr Pax?"

"Different?"

"I think you understand."

Themistius looked at the bodyguards stood a little way from the table. They had their backs to the booth and didn't appear to be listening. "Well yes. I suppose I have been feeling more fatigued than usual," he said quietly. "Work must come first of course."

"It is not your dedication I am questioning."

It was hard to look at the mask and the dark eyes behind it. Themistius shifted his gaze again toward the window. The rain was heavier now so that everything outside had become a blur. His look returned to Veles. Themistius took a breath. "With respect sir, what is it that you *are* questioning?" If I have failed you then please tell me where I have fallen short. I have only ever worked for the greatness of Atlantis."

Veles sat back against the red padded seat and laughed. "Your failure to capture Pax is not altogether unexpected. The disaster last night only confirms that my suspicions are correct. The Kosmics are rising, as is foretold in their ancient legends. There is some powerful force abroad in this land and it means to sweep away all before it, all that I have done with Atlantis." He thudded his scarred hand onto the table, making his spoon chime in the glass. Themistius heard the loose skin flickering against the mask as Veles breathed angrily. Then came a chuckle. "It is not you, Themistius," the Emperor went on. "You are merely an ignorant part of a complex mechanism you cannot possibly have any true understanding of."

Themistius dropped his head. "I will find Pax for you."

"It is not only Pax. It is the Kosmics. Something is happening. Pax, I believe, is the spearhead of this great change. The beginning. But I think you know that already. You understand this change, don't you?"

"I do not follow sir?"

"You have been touched by Pax and experienced his abilities. You have tasted his power first hand have you not?"

Themistius only nodded, unable to deceive. A week before they had raided a Kosmic stronghold. He had chased the mysterious Peregrine Pax himself. They had fought. Pax got away.

"There is more, isn't there?" Veles' dark eyes fixed him.

Themistius did not know how to answer. He was not sure what he should tell his leader.

"I can see it in your eyes Themistius. You are not well and have not been since your encounter with Pax. Tell me, isn't it as if you have woken from some terrible fever only to find the sense of delirium has stayed with you?"

Themistius began to shake. No longer could he keep hold of all the feelings that were churning within. His eyes watered. "Perhaps you are right." He tried to clamp down on his emotions, wiping the moisture away with the back of his hand. "I have probably picked up some infection from that dog, Pax. He was a dirty creature." Again, Themistius hoped he sounded convincing.

Veles shook his head. "I know as well as you that it is not quite that simple. This change is more profound. You are wrestling with it. Your mind is in anguish."

Themistius began to stutter a response but Veles only spoke over him.

"You have inadvertently become a most valuable object. The continuing effects of your encounter with Pax need to be studied and monitored."

Themistius could smell Veles; a mixture of something clinical mingled with something stale and pungent like the bed sheets of a dead man. It made his stomach turn. "How do you know these things about Pax? Our intelligence is so limited. How can I make progress in locating him if information is being withheld? We know his name and we believe he is from the Plains of Aykona, a breeding ground for subversives."

Veles laughed again. "I understand your rage and frustration. But now you are more important to me than ever before."

"I do not understand," Themistius said dumbly shaking his head.

Veles turned to the men guarding their table. "Get everyone out. Everyone."

The two large, suited men did as they were instructed. The other agents in the café quickly moved to the doors. In a moment the place was empty. Only Veles and Themistius remained.

"Do you know," Veles began, "what is known of my life prior to my political successes?"

"No sir," Themistius replied. "I'm afraid I don't."

"That is because I have made sure only my closest advisors within the pyramid of government know anything of it."

Themistius nodded whilst his mind whirred. Was the moment come that he had long expected? Was Veles about to have him killed? The Emperor's brutality not only toward the people but to those who had failed him was well known. If this was where his life was to be ended could anything be done? Themistius wondered. Could he kill Veles before Veles killed him? Even if he could, what then? Agents would be on him immediately and his life would be over anyway – at least, however, he would not be another of Veles' sacrifices to the greatness of Atlantis. He would take the pompous maniac with him.

Veles picked up the steak knife from the table and began to casually clean his finger nails with it, eyes still fixed on Themistius. "Until I was nearly thirty I hadn't amounted to much. At that time the council of elders ran things."

"I remember those times," Themistius nodded. It seemed so long ago to him – to everyone.

"I had drifted for many years – fruit picking here and there, a string of dead end jobs. Finally I joined the Atlantean Guard, as it was known then. After basic training my first post was up in the North West peninsular, a desolate and feral place even then. I had been up there about three months when one evening I was given the task of responding to a report of some lunatic running wild at a spot called Tunga Bay. The locals had been frightened by his wild looks and babbling speech. It was assumed he was an escaped prisoner on the run."

As he listened to his chief, Themistius looked at the mask and the eyes looking out from it. He tried to read those eyes; arrogant? Deceptive? Candid?

"I went to the beach." A small pile of skin and dirt was collecting on the table where Veles cleaned his nails. "It did not take me long to find the wild man. Only he was not wild, simply scared. He had dug himself into the dunes, rocking and mumbling. I could make no sense of what he was saying. I dragged him from his bunker and tried to communicate but it was no use. He was a man of no more than thirty himself." Veles stopped, sat back and absently gazed about the café, reliving the scene in his mind. "At the time I remember wishing I was back at HQ, sat by the fire with my feet up, rather than hunting escaped mental patients on some bitterly cold finger of sand sticking out into an icy ocean. However, if I had not been on that beach I might never have become Emperor."

Themistius watched Veles closely. As he listened to the story he was aware that Veles could very easily lean over the table and screw the blade through his eyes and deep into his brain. Veles would even use his blood as sauce for his ice cream. Themistius stole a glance behind the Emperor to see if any agent had crept back in but none had. There was only the empty tables and large panoramic windows that looked toward the mountains, made dreamy by the rain. His eyes shifted back to Veles who was watching Themistius just as closely.

"I would be offended," the Emperor told him, "if you *did* trust me."

"Sir, I was…"

Veles silenced him with a raised hand. "You think that when my story ends, so will your life? On the contrary; if you allow me to finish you will find it quite enlightening. Your life is not in danger, I assure you." The skin of his face clacked against the mask. "If it were, you would already be dead," he added.

Themistius nodded. He felt an overwhelming hatred for the man opposite him. This hate seemed to come from some new part of him; the part that had been growing since his encounter with Peregrine Pax.

"At first," the Emperor continued, "I did not restrain him. There was no need – he was weak and disorientated and without manacles was easier to drag across the beach. I had tried to communicate with him but got nowhere with it. I knew, however, he was not just some crazy hobo. He had a look in his eyes that I had never seen the like of before. Just as we were almost off the sand, he stopped and became a dead weight. As I tried to force him up he lurched for me, knocking us both to the ground. We fought but his strength was greater than his appearance suggested. As we scuffled he grabbed my head with his hands. That's when it happened."

"It?" But Themistius understood.

"An experience I have never fully recovered from." Veles looked at his hands. "Whoever this person was, he had powers and abilities beyond the Kosmics and their silly dirt magic."

Themistius leaned closer. "Tell me sir. Tell me what happened, how it made you feel?"

"It is possible you are the only person who might understand." Veles paused. "I experienced a blinding light, as if the marrow of my bones would burn from the intensity. I felt a pain almost exquisite in the way it pushed at the edges of ecstasy."

"There was more wasn't there?" Themistius recalled his own fight with Pax.

"Yes." Veles reached out his scarred hand and with his finger, gently touched Themistius on the forehead. "There was no separation between my consciousness and that of the rest of Atlantis. I was part of its flux and flow. In that moment I no longer existed and it felt blissful and pure. For just that moment there was no longer 'this' or 'that', or 'me' and 'them.' There was only a bright, white, silent unity. Then it was gone." He took his hand away.

"I have felt this too," Themistius told him. "It was Pax wasn't it? He is special."

"I believe so." Veles waited, his eyes locked on Themistius, seeming to register his every twitch and bead of sweat. "We have both experienced his power, though the effects have been quite different. You have not suffered in the way that I did. I do not know how long I was on the beach," Veles went on. "Eventually I was found and taken to hospital. Had I not been in uniform they would not have been able to identify me. My encounter with Pax had left most of my body severely burnt and disfigured. No one could say exactly how the wounds had been caused. I was in the hospital for six months and unconscious for three of them. It is since then that I have had a series of prosthetic masks."

"And Pax gave you something else, didn't he?" Themistius said in a whisper.

Veles leaned back in his seat. "I think of it as a gift. Beyond the scars I was left with a stronger mind and greater physical strength. I was no longer like every other Atlantean. I had changed from a rat to a wolf. My thoughts were sharper and quicker and I rose through the political arm of the Atlantean Guard, into the high echelons of the elite without struggle. My mask made me feared but it was the speed of my ruthless, calculating mind that always ensured my success. At last I took control and dispensed with the elders."

"But my experience is different," Themistius told him. "I have but one small scar." He looked at his hand again. "I have only felt sick and disorientated."

"Perhaps." Veles was once again remote; any emotion stirred up by his recollections had vanished. "It takes time for things to manifest. You and I are the only people that are known to have been marked by Pax. There may be others across Atlantis, hiding from the light. Now that I have found you, we are in a way like…" Veles searched for the word…"Brothers. For years I have hunted for Pax. He had become a phantom in my mind, sometimes I even doubted what had happened and wondered if there had been any wild man on the beach at all. Now though, I have you. So, you are of great value to me and to Atlantis."

Themistius closed his eyes and hoped he projected sincerity. "I will always serve you and the greater good of Atlantis. If I have angered you with my actions and my failure last night then I am sorry."

"Pax was in control last night. There was little you could have done."

Themistius was surprised. "You think that Pax is leading the insurgents? That he planted the bomb?"

Veles nodded. "He is involved, either directly or indirectly and he is not working alone."

Themistius could no longer stand to have Veles' white mask scrutinize him. He wished her were alone so that he could process all he had been told. He stood and walked toward the large windows. "It is all so strange, so hard to understand," he told the Emperor. "I have been feeling so out of sorts these past few days. What is it you want me to do?" He looked toward the mountains and imagined being a thousand miles away from everything.

"When you return to the capital there will be a team of doctors waiting to run tests on you. It may be possible to discern the type of symptoms you have and how they might develop. It may also tell us something of Pax. Anything we discover could lead us closer to him. We must work tirelessly now. The Kosmics are rising and the very existence of Atlantis is threatened. They must be annihilated."

"Sir." Themistius turned from the panorama back to Veles. "What is your belief? Who do you think that Pax is, to have the power he has?"

Veles stood. "That is the important question, isn't it?" He walked toward Themistius. "I have given much thought to it since my first meeting with him. In the ancient legends there are many prophecies that a great priest will one day come and lead people into light, back to an understanding of the Kosmic flow. Pax may be an incarnation of these legends. I am sure that is what the Kosmics believe. I think he may be a quirk of nature – I do not know but I want him found and dissected until we understand everything about him." Veles placed his arm around Themistius and began walking him toward the door. Themistius smelt his odour again.

"This is so much to understand," Themistius confessed. "What you have said is fantastical and yet I see its truth."

"Good. I would hate to think your mistrust of me ran so very deep. That would be most unfortunate."

Themistius shook his head. "I thought I had failed."

They stopped at the threshold.

"Go back to the capital then," Veles told him. "Do not worry about Pax for the time being. I shall keep you informed of developments. You must allow the doctors to do their tests on you."

Both men looked into each other's eyes and nodded. The door of the Mountain View Café was opened by an agent from outside and Themistius found himself standing in the rain. He stood for a moment, no more. He looked toward the far mountainside and its newly carved message in giant letters: ATLANTIS FOR ALL. The words made him shudder. He walked away feeling sick.

Ms ALIVE

There was an idle rhythm of bedsheets dangling from washing lines, like sails for the sun. Annabelle looked out from the window of the bus. Every garden they passed had its washing line in bloom and the morning sun was caught in a desultory dance with shirts and sheets; an idle rhythm dangling, the bus sweeping past, making the long grass of the verge and the spent cow parsley nod frantically.

She looked down at her hand as it nervously tapped upon the metal sill of the bus window. She noticed the words 'get paid' had been scratched into the magnesium grey of the paint.

Get paid, in jagged letters. There were other scratches along the sill but it was those two words that caught her eye amongst the swear words, the initials in hearts and the badly carved swastikas. Annabelle wondered absently what became of whoever had made those marks and why they had made them. Everywhere, she thought, people trying to leave a mark, scratching at paint.

She checked her watch. The bus had left Bristol two hours before and now the big lanes of motorway had withered to become this Devonshire country road, with its thriving verges and proximity to stone walls and oncoming cars pulling caravans. It was so narrow that several times Annabelle thought the bus was going to hit something from the other direction. It was just as she tried to guess how much further it could be, they slowed down and then stopped with a hiss.

"Girl who wanted the Spratt Hotel?" the driver called along the aisle.

"Yes!" Annabelle called back. "Thank you." Hastily she grabbed her things.

No one else wanted the stop and the bus quickly groaned and hissed itself off along the road leaving the girl with a short walk along a pathway toward a large, white hotel with blue Art Deco lines tracing its edges.

In her head, as the name suggested, the Spratt Hotel had been small. It was not. Striking in its whiteness. Imposing from its setting near the clifftop above the cove. It may have had a faded grandeur but there was still more of the grand than the fade. It almost glistened in the morning light and Annabelle thought of the bedsheets on the washing lines once more.

She stopped to check her phone but there were no messages of good luck; but then no one really knew. Out of necessity she had made the decision to leave very quickly. It did not matter, she told herself. She would simply let her father know the following day when she had gotten settled.

As she drew closer to the entrance the sea air suddenly caught her nose and through the tennis courts she could see it, the ocean, a vast blue far darker than the sky. She passed expensive looking cars and expensive looking people and went inside to the reception. She was directed to the Primrose Lounge where the entertainment manager could be found.

"What's your name?" he asked from the centre of the dancefloor. He had been staring up at a lighting rig and hadn't heard her properly when she introduced herself.

"Annabelle Alive," she told him again. There seemed to be even more of an echo now that he was looking right at her.

"Right." He nodded in a way that suggested he had been expecting her and she felt some relief. "That a stage name?" he asked.

"No. It's just my name."

"Great." He nodded. Then his face changed and became stiffer. "So Annabelle, ever had any experience working behind a bar?"

"I think there might have been a mistake," she smiled, at last putting down the three bags that contained all she owned. "I'm a dancer. I'm here for the position of a dancer and a dance instructor. It was all confirmed last week."

"Things have changed," he told her and looked around like he wanted to lean against something. "I mean there have been some alterations that have had to be made. We no longer need a dancer, at least not entirely."

Annabelle looked confused.

"You see," the entertainment manager went on, walking from the dancefloor. "We only need a dancer for two nights a week now. It was supposed to be more but…" he shrugged.

"Things have changed," she finished for him.

"That's right. But we also need a new member for the bar team. You'll be in here," he added, "just serving drinks though, four days a week."

She looked over at the bar. Dark. Shuttered.

"We thought you could fill the role. You said on the phone you were making a new start down here. That's right?"

"Yes," she told him looking about the rest of the Primrose Lounge for the first time. Elegant. Faded. "And there's really no positions for a dancer? Full time?" She tried to smile the way she had smiled five minutes before.

The manager raised his palms as if feeling for rain. "This is it. Take it or leave it."

Annabelle suddenly felt heavy in her legs while her head became light. "But a room is still included?" she asked. Without the room she was sunk.

"Yeah. Everything is the same." He looked at her bags. "I'm sorry we couldn't let you know sooner. It was sort of last minute."

"That's fine." It would have to be, she told herself. "I'll take it – as long as I can still dance a little."

"Oh sure," the manager smiled. "If things change we can talk again." He moved to pick up one of her bags. "Let me show you to your quarters and then I can orientate you a little. Look – just see how it goes. Give it a month at least."

Annabelle followed him. "Why a month?" she asked.

He stopped at the doorway. "That's when you get paid."

VULPECULAN CONQUEST

With my wife having left me six months before (after several explosive rows where we screamed at each other about our disappointments) and my publisher pacing up and down on my balls every day, waiting for me to deliver the manuscript I had been promising, the one that would complete the trilogy, with all that, I decided to get out of the city and find some space where I could think.

My old friend, Grant Sullivan, happened to call around this time and had to listen to me whining about everything. He was firm. "You have to finish the trilogy," he told me. "People have to know how it ends."

"Maybe." I felt sick of it. Sick of everything.

"Don't be an idiot." There was clear frustration in his voice. "You can't stop at two. Do the job, finish and move on. Otherwise it's goodbye career."

"Uh-huh."

Grant was a successful web developer and had achieved success on his own terms, starting out with nothing. That's probably why I listened to him more than others. People either envied him or dismissed him but I had known him long enough to see through all his bravado; I knew he was right.

"I have an idea," he said. There was a pause and I could hear the ice chinking in his glass. "I bought a piece of land out in the country back in April. Haven't been there yet but it has this lovely old farm house. It's only a couple of hours from you. I'll speak with my property manager. You can stay there for a while.

It's right out in the country – a little village called Low Scaraby. Go there and finish your book, get some space. Relax a little."

So I did. I gathered together some clothes without really thinking and tossed them into the back of my old Volvo. I sent an email to my agent, explaining things in the vaguest of detail, and then I left. I set the GPS with the address Grant had given me and I drove feeling relieved to be leaving the concrete brutality of the city behind me. I really hoped that during the drive into emptier and emptier space, the creative portion of my mind would begin lifting rocks, hoping to find underneath some fat, juicy ideas for part three of my trilogy; the one my publisher was screaming for.

Parts one and two of *Vulpeculan Conquest* had sold well – much better than my agent or publisher had anticipated and in the two years since the second instalment ever more readers had discovered it and told their friends. There were now even whispers of film rights. Things were good, or would have been if not for my divorce and the fact that I had written myself into a dark room where nothing was certain; was that a light switch or the pin of a grenade? John Dustin Wilson might have '*reinvigorated the alien invasion of Earth genre for the twenty first century,*' according to The Guardian, but sadly, John Dustin Wilson had no clue how he had done it and was out of fresh ideas.

Grant's estates manager, whose name was Mr Hewish, had left the key in the eave of the porch. It was in exactly the spot the email said it would be, though it looked as if not a soul had been there for quite some time.

The farmhouse sat on the top of a gentle hill and looked down upon a patchwork of meadows and fields. Beyond the farmland was more farmland and then a curtain of trees. No internet. No phone. I breathed and gave my crotch a deep post-drive scratch. This space could be what I needed; what

Vulpeculan Conquest Part III needed. I unloaded the car, found a bedroom and slept.

I had been at my adytum for a few days. It was basic; the only source of water was a hand pump in the courtyard or a stream at the end of the long track that led from the road to the house. Electricity came from a generator in one of the outbuildings and any cooking I did was on a stove. My first full day at the place was spent discovering all this stuff and setting up a little writing desk in the yard next to the house. I consulted a map and drove out to the nearest town, a small place about ten miles from Low Scaraby called Bilsby. It had a mini supermarket open until 11pm, a petrol station and a great view of nothing more than fields and the faint white stalks of wind turbines on the coast about thirty miles away.

Those initial days I was finding a rhythm, perhaps like a boxer in the early rounds. I stalked the courtyard and the outbuildings each morning, pushing and poking at my ideas, testing my reach, my strength.

The courtyard was comprised of two barns divided into different workshops. Inside each was nothing but dust and bird shit. There was one building I would not explore. It was closed off by a blackened, crumbling pine door on which someone had painted a red X. That was enough for me. Each time I got close I began to feel unsteady. Not on my feet so much as in my head. It was probably where the herbicides and other poisons had been kept and I stayed away. After the courtyard I trotted down to the stream and bathed before the day's heat got too ferocious, then I'd set myself up at the desk and faced my audience of meadow flowers. I shouted random lines out, descriptions of characters, segments of plot. I tried to write and tried to pretend there was no pressure on it.

It was on such a morning, just as I was about to start writing, when there began an awful crying sound. I thought I had heard something similar the night before as I lay in bed. A rhythmic pulsing cry. Now it had started again. It was not yet nine but the day was already hot. In the daylight it was a guttural whine that pierced the air and seemed to echo up from the earth and rebound against the farmhouse. After a few minutes I realised it was coming from the dyke along the edge of a nearby field, sheltered by trees. I decided to investigate and went scrambling down the dirt bank and into its cool, fetid shade. As my eyes adjusted to the subsoil gloom I saw the body of a fox lying like an abandoned lover, its flank a large wound of matted blood and innards. It was impossible to tell how the animal had received its injury. Perhaps it was from a gunshot or the attack of another predator. The poor creature's eyes flickered open on hearing my presence. Its senses were dulled and ready for death. I waited with it for some minutes. It cried and moaned and breathed heavily. Finally I could not stand it any longer. Hunting along the length of the ditch I found a smooth rounded stone, dark in colour and a perfect size to be grasped in the hand. I took it back to where the fox was still murmuring its final testament to the undomesticated world. I raised the stone and struck it hard over the animal's head. There was blood and silence.

I left its carcass in the ditch and threw a few leaves over it. As I returned to the house, feeling out of sorts from the experience of being murderer, undertaker and chief mourner, I saw the letter waiting for me. It was in a plain envelope and had been placed at the front door so that I could not help but see it. I looked about me but there was no one to be seen and no vehicle disappearing back down the track. I gazed at the envelope and the envelope gazed at me. Only my agent knew I was here and I had told him not to contact me for at least two weeks. It could have been Mr Hewish, the estate manager, but I doubted he would leave silly notes. Finally I could ignore it no longer and tore it open.

A single piece of folded paper with a coffee stain in its bottom right corner. The headed notepaper had come from the Bilsby Motel. It read:

Uncle Tony has thrown me out. You know what he can be like. Now I'm in this motel and it's full of bugs and there are stains from god knows what. I don't have much money. Can I stay with you? I know it has been a while but I can help with any work you need doing, just until Uncle Tony comes round. Maybe you could speak to him? I hate to ask this of you but I have nowhere else I can go.

Jocelyn

I read it several times over. I did not know any Uncle Tony. I did not know anyone called Jocelyn. She was certainly mistaken – whoever she was. I did not know how the letter had arrived but it was not meant for me. Perhaps it was some sort of set up from my wife. I wasn't sure exactly but it would be some way for her to demand more from me and to humiliate me. Maybe even my publishers were involved. Again I didn't know how but I wouldn't have put it passed them – no good bastards. Then I saw another connection; the Vulpeculans. In part two of the trilogy a small unit of Vulpeculan combatants take human form as part of their infiltration of Earth. Could this be something similar? They knew about my indiscretion on the book tour. They knew my wife's reaction. Were they goading me? Had they injured the fox and left it for me to find?

I brooded all day and tried to work these things out. It was early evening by the time I armed myself with a knife from the kitchen and stomped back to the ditch to take a closer look at the fox.

It was gone. There was nothing, not even the bloodied stone I had struck it with. If the carcass had been picked at by crows and other scavengers, I would have expected some evidence to remain after just a few hours but there was nothing. It was as I trudged back through the courtyard, feeling shaken, that I saw the fox corpse in front of the outbuilding with a red X on its door, sat as if it had just wandered in and plonked itself down. I approached cautiously. As I bent to touch the dead animal I was punched by a sound that forced the breath from my body and the knife from my hand. It was the noise that static fuzz would make if it turned to liquid, was poured over screaming children and then set alight. I collapsed in pain.

"Enter," said a voice cutting through my paroxysm. "Come inside so that you may see. Open the door and enter." It was not like any voice I had heard before but I understood it. I could understand its modulations and felt my bones and skin as the medium rendering the vibrations clear.

"Enter," it told me again impatiently. "John Dustin Wilson. Enter."

I pulled myself up and did as I was told, all sense of logic suppressed. The rusted handle felt like wire wool in my palm as I twisted it and swung open the door. The evening light stepped in with me but the warmth it still possessed turned cold as it touched the skulls. Three walls of skulls, their black eye sockets glaring at me. Skulls stacked high as the timber joists above.

Ivory domes of various shades, housing eyes of the same deep black. Long dead animals of disparate kinds, harvested and hoarded.

"John Dustin Wilson." I felt the voice within and without again, amplified by the ossuary in front of me. I trembled but had no strength to turn and run. I knew running would do no good anyway.

"Bring more," said the voice. "You can bring more. Continue the chain. Turn the circle."

"More what?" I asked. "What is it you want?"

"John Dustin Wilson, bring flesh and the circle will turn."

I fell backwards out of the doorway, tripping over the dead fox. I crawled in the dirt and eventually staggered upright. The voice was still inside of me. Demanding. I tried to think but thinking seemed redundant and ancient. I walked in broken circles, clawing at the air. Then I got in my car, fell into the seat, started the engine and drove.

During the entire journey into Bilsby the voice remained in my head, constantly repeating its demand for flesh. It was nearly dark when I turned into the supermarket car park, my mind made up. I grabbed a trolley and headed for the aisle labelled 'MEATS.' The voice seemed to sense my proximity to its desire and the mantra in my head increased its volume.

As I threw random chunks of meat into the trolley I felt like a contestant on a nightmare gameshow.

"Can I help you?" A tired looking supervisor had appeared from the dairy section. He looked concerned but not surprised – a veteran of the nightshift. I told him I was fine. He nodded, unconvinced, and filed me under 'harmless.'

I got back to the farmhouse as quickly as I could, carrying my purchases to the outbuilding. I brought a torch with me and moved its beams across the rows of skulls sat like jars on a shelf.

"At your feet is a trapdoor," the voice told me. "Open it and throw down the flesh."

Kicking away dirt and straw I saw the wooden hatch. Again I did as I was told, pulling it open and emptying the meat into its darkness. I threw in the carcass of the fox too. When I had finished I closed the hatch and collapsed. Briefly, the voice had been silenced. Then it came again, calmer.

"Leave me now. We must both rest. Tomorrow we will begin." After that the voice was silent.

Confused and exhausted I lumbered back to the house and passed out.

*

Jocelyn must have arrived early in the morning. As I went downstairs bright sunlight was streaming in from everywhere and the radio was playing in the kitchen. I turned at the last step and saw a young woman with hair dark like a bottle of red wine. She wore a cotton dress patterned with swallows darting from her shoulders to her knees.

"I let myself in," she told me trying not to look anxious.

"Jocelyn?"

She nodded.

"You've made a mistake," I said walking into the kitchen and past her.

"You got my letter?" she asked.

I stopped when I saw the table. Fried bread, fried eggs, bacon, fresh coffee, all laid out.

"I like a good breakfast in the morning," she explained, pulling a chair back for me to sit down. "I think it's important. Don't you?"

"I don't want guests," I told her flatly. The food smelt good. I had woken with a huge appetite. "You can't stay," I added, not looking at her. I sat, gazing at the bacon and the coffee.

She stood in front of me, brushing invisible dirt from the swallows of her dress. "You should eat," she said gently. "You look ready to eat the head from a rat."

She looked hungry too and I told her she should sit down. As we ate we talked. I had never known a breakfast to taste so good. I softened and told her I was a writer. She thought she remembered reading one of my books, she said she enjoyed science fiction. It was stupid flattery and yet I couldn't help but like her. I didn't understand how anyone could turn her out. I said she could stay a few days, then after we finished eating she insisted on clearing things away.

"Why don't you go on out to your desk and write?" she suggested.

I went and turned to a blank page in my notebook. It was then the voice returned. The same voice as the night before but now somehow rooted down within me.

"I can help you," said the voice.

“How?” I whispered and glanced back. Jocelyn was busy humming along to the radio, oblivious to my muttering.

“You are here to write. I can help you write.”

“Write what?”

“What you need.” The voice waited as if counting my breaths. “To complete your trilogy. To explain the final triumph and meaning of the Vulpeculan people’s colonization of Earth.”

“Yes,” I said a little fearful. “That is what will happen.”

“John Dustin Wilson, it has already begun.”

I picked up my pen and wrote. For hours I wrote with nothing but the voice in my mind, leading me into the Vulpeculan labyrinth so that I could see their desperate existence among the stars. All through the morning and into the afternoon I wrote until I must have fallen asleep. When Jocelyn reappeared it was evening. She held out a glass of lemonade. "You have been busy today," she smiled.

I knew then I could finish my trilogy. The weight of it would be lifted just as long as I fed the Vulpeculan entity.

"I must have meat," was the background hum. "You will bring it to me."

A routine began. During the day I wrote – some of the best stuff I had ever written – and then in the late afternoon or early evening Jocelyn would appear. We would take a walk together along the meadow and talk about the places we had been and books and all kinds of trivial stuff. I even told her about my wife and the one night stand I had on my book tour and how it had led to our breakup. I told her I had been stupid.

"It's not because you are a man and you are weak or have male urges," she told me. "I hate it when people speak so dismissively." She looked me straight in the eye. “It is because you are human,” she smiled. “We fuck up.”

I liked our walks together and if I ever came across a dead animal of some kind I would remember its location and return later in the night. In the darkness I began to feed the trapdoor a mixture of processed meat from the supermarket and carrion I had found. I fed the voice and the words kept coming. Brilliant words. My best words. After I had poured the meat down the trapdoor I would stay a while, with the skulls and their energy.

“Are there more of you coming?” I asked one night.

“More?”

“To complete the conquest. To make things better.”

“There are enough already.” The voice sounded tired. “Only more energy, more belief is required.”

“I believe,” I told it.

"And the final part of your trilogy will help others to believe also. You feed me and I can feed you. You understand don't you?"

I nodded and reaching out I gently touched the skulls. I ran my fingers along them. They felt warm.

"That girl," said the voice. "The one who has come here. Imagine the power she would provide instead of this processed and rotten filth I get. Consider the power of your writing then. If you brought her to me our revolution would be magnificent."

"Yes," I said, remembering the day I first opened the door with the red X. "How long has this place been here?" I asked.

"What does it matter to you?"

"I just…"

"Do you ask how long the rocks have been? Or rivers? Or the moon?

"No." Its temper was always just below the surface but I had become restless to understand. "This book I am writing," I went on. "Isn't it for both of us?"

The skulls maintained their lifeless gaze while the rafters above creaked from the day's heat. The voice was silent. I could feel it though, just like a phantom hat you still feel on your head after you have taken it off.

After a moment it spoke. "Do not question me. Do not speak with me anymore until you have brought that girl to me. Then we will finish this and the book will be written."

"I cannot do that," I told it. "Not Jocelyn."

"You will do it. You are weak. Bring her."

I left, slamming the door. I was not angry, only scared because I was a coward and could hide nothing from the voice. I felt the Vulpeculan claws deep within me; in my blood, in my bones, in my breath. It had control. I paced round and round, feeling it gnawing at my thoughts.

"Bring me the girl. Bring me the girl." That was the mantra, like a distant dog barking only for me.

I did not dare return to the house. Jocelyn was in there, sleeping and vulnerable. Finally I locked myself in the car and curled up on the back seat, pulling a blanket over me, trying to imagine a new diorama for my thoughts to be sealed in. I thought of so many things from my life, good and bad, just to try and block out the voice. Nothing worked for long. Like a sore or a splinter eventually it would announce itself to my senses, sending all my other pictures into nothing. I sweated and shivered with the malevolent static prodding at me relentlessly.

"Bring me the girl. Bring me the girl. Finish your book. Bring me the girl."

It was some time around dawn when I heard a tapping on the window. It was Jocelyn. "What's going on?" she asked. "Why are you sleeping in your car? I thought you had disappeared."

"I can't be with you now," I told her. The voice was immediately louder in my head. I tried to shout over it. "You need to leave."

"What is going on? What's wrong with you?"

Even as I tried to resist I knew that I had already made the decision. I was already enjoying the moment when all the pretence was pushed aside and the guilt had shrivelled away and perished. I closed my eyes, gripping at the upholstery of the seat, trying not to move and yet I was already dragging her by the hair across the courtyard. "You should never have appeared," I told her. Only part of me meant it but it didn't matter. It was too late. In only a second I had opened the door and knocked her to the ground. Before she could react in any meaningful way I was taking her to the room of skulls. Of course she began screaming and kicking but that only seemed to justify my actions more. I wanted her gone. I wanted her to shut up and I wanted to finish my writing.

"That's it," said the voice. "Give her to me. Throw her down so that I can ingest and assimilate her. Our words will be magnificent now."

"Please," Jocelyn begged. "Why are you doing this? What's happened to you? Stop!"

I wasn't going to stop. I couldn't. The voice was too strong and loud. Sacrificing her could set me free. That was enough. "I'm sorry," I told her. "I have to."

The Vulpeculan voice was throbbing in my mind, closing off any other thoughts or sensations. Jocelyn was shouting at me and begging me to stop. Once inside the room I pulled the trapdoor open. Jocelyn was struggling so much I had to hit her, stunning her enough to throw her down into the dark. She groaned when she hit the floor, covered as it was in the remains of animals. Just as she began to scream I slammed the door shut and pulled the bolt.

"That's it," the voice said gleefully. "You understand what needs to be done. John Dustin Wilson understands the sacrifices needed to be a great writer."

I nodded but only felt confused and sick at what I had done.

"Leave me now," the voice went on more calmly. "I need more time. This evening we will write."

I left but could not return to the farmhouse, not straightaway. Instead I stumbled down the track, toward the sun that was beginning to rise in the sky. I wondered if the Vulpeculan sun was rising in an unknown sky somewhere very distant from all of this. I went along in a haze, staggered by what I had so easily done, and eventually came to the ditch where the dead fox had been. I understood then that the fox had been the beginning of it all. It had been the herald of the Vulpeculan's arrival. Once more I scrambled down the dirt bank, into the shade that had not yet shrugged off the pre-dawn cool. I was determined to discover something, perhaps it was my other self I longed to find, anything that might tell me more about what had taken hold of me.

I stopped when I saw it. The carcass of a dead animal. Though severely maimed and distorted I could see the creature had a long tail and a dog-like face. I got close to it, planting my knees in the mud. A fox. But the same fox I had found half dead? Hadn't I fed it to the abyss of the trapdoor? There was enough of this animal left to see that it had been injured along its flank and sat next to it in the dirt was a rounded stone with dried blood smeared upon it.

I got up and pulled myself from the shadow and soil like a ghoul rising from the grave. As I ran I screamed for the voice. I screamed to be answered all the way back to the ossuary.

The house of bones had a door. A weather beaten old thing with rusted hinges but now there was no red X. There was nothing at all except the marks of time on an old door. I stood staring at it, trying to hear the voice.

"Answer me!" I screamed, wrenching the door open. I screamed again and began pulling at the stacks of skulls. I snarled and I pulled the skulls down but as they tumbled they turned to fruit crates. I called out for the voice but the only reply was the tumbling clatter of wooden crates. A pile formed at my feet; boxes with an antique accumulation of dirt from the fields and undecipherable labels, cracked and peeled from season upon season of use. Kicking them out of the way I found the handle for the trapdoor and pulled it open. Down in its shade was nothing but straw and stillness.

I fell backwards, out into the light. There was no voice. I could not feel it inside me anywhere. When I breathed I only felt my lungs, no longer breathing with the weight of another upon them. The burning gulps of panic were all my own.

I charged to the farmhouse. Inside everything was quiet. In the kitchen there were no traces of our meal from the night before, no plates on the draining board, no radio set upon the worktop. Upstairs, in my room, was the unmade bed and a pile of my clothes. Across the hall, where Jocelyn slept, the room was empty; there was an uncovered mattress and a wardrobe in which all that hung were bare coat hangers.

I stood in her room a long time. Even her smell had vanished and there was no vase of wildflowers that she had picked from the meadow and placed on the windowsill.

As I went downstairs I tried to gather the fragments of my thoughts into something coherent. It was only as I stepped outside again that I thought of my writing. I saw my notebook on the desk, its pages fluttering with the breeze. Above all the frenzy I knew I had been writing. Everything else might have vanished like some elaborate magician's trick but not those words. They remained. Even without the voice or the skulls or even the girl, there were the words I had written. I was certain of it. At my desk, facing out to the track that led to the road and to Low Scaraby and to Bilsby, I had sat there for hours and I had written. So many words. My best words.

Slowly, I went to my desk and looked down at the notebook. Its pages had been blown to the last leaf as if the wind had read it. I looked at the pen sat idly next to the book. My wife had bought it for me in New York. It had a perfectly balanced weight that signified its quality. Yes, I was certain, with that pen I had sat and I had written my best stuff in years. I picked up the notebook, my hand shaking as I turned it to the beginning.

WORMS OF DEATH

I saw my neighbour pacing around his front door and around his driveway in tight circles. His name is John. My wife calls him Fester.

John must be around fifty something. He's balding and has a shaved head and his front teeth stick out a little and rest on his bottom lip when he is thinking.

When he sees me he says, "I've dealt with them." I notice a small propane torch in his hand. He goes back to pacing, head down. "I warned the little bastards," his front teeth appear and a grin flashes across his face.

I look where he's looking. "Dealt with what?"

“Maggots.” He looks about him on the driveway. “All those fucking maggots.”

I don’t see any maggots. I don’t even see any burnt remains of maggots which I imagine would look like blackened rice or dark unpopped popcorn.

“You had maggots?” I say.

“Yeah.” He points over to where his bins stand. “Started over there. Must’ve been something dead or a piece of meat or something. Bad sign.”

I look around more closely.

“Then they were at my door,” he goes on. “Wriggling about near the drainpipe. I tried bleach at first but it didn’t seem to do no good.”

I remembered last year when I came home and found John trying to open his front door. He was puffing and panting and cursing the kids who must’ve superglued his lock. When I went over to help I could see that he’d jammed the wrong key in upside down. There wasn’t any superglue.

"When did you see these maggots?" I ask him.

"Yesterday. Didn't you see them? I didn't want them to spread to you. Then today I found more. Worms of death I call them. So that was it. I said – it's blowtorch time."

I began to wonder how long he had been pacing about. The day before I had seen his sister, grim faced. That was how she often looked but I suppose it would be. She went round to keep an eye on John. From what I knew she had bought the house and took care of everything. You see, John was losing his marbles. It was sad for it to happen to him at a relatively young age but, his sister told me, it had been the same for their father. Whenever she came by she was dressed very neatly but always looked tired and mirthless. I put her age at a year or two younger than poor old John.

"If you see any maggots on your property," he says looking at me, "just give me a shout." He shook the canister at me with a smile.

"Will do," I nodded.

He turned his attention to the sky. "Looks like it will be a nice evening. Might get the motorbike out and go for a ride."

His sister had sold his bike about six months before. I nodded and told him to take care.

I didn't see John for a few days, then on Thursday I saw his sister coming out of the front door. "I've had to move him into care," she told me looking downcast. "In the last week or two something really changed with him."

"I'm sorry," I replied. I felt sad that I would no longer see Fester, pottering about in his garden, staring at his roses.

"It's the best place for him," she said with a nod.

I watched her walk to her car and as I did I saw something on John's driveway. Then I saw something near his door. I got down on my hands and knees to have a closer look.

Maggots. A dozen maggots or more. Blindly wriggling and twitching as if freshly unfolded from some dark crack in the earth.

"Wait!" I called out to John's sister. "Didn't you see all of these?" But it was too late and she had driven away.

THE NETHERBEAST

"…I was thirteen at the time so this would have been in 1990. That August there was an incredible heatwave. A couple of Low Scaraby's older residents had even kicked the bucket because it was so hot, but for me and my mates it was a great time. We tramped about the countryside during the holidays and the days went on forever. Most of the kids from the village went swimming in Nether Pond. It was the best way to keep cool and have fun.

"The summer of 1990 was also significant for me because of Hayley Brown; my first girlfriend. On this particular evening we had arranged to meet and go to Nether Pond together. I think the idea was that we would go skinny dipping. That night though there was a fire up at the Hudson farm. Straw was tinder dry and it had caught light in one of the barns, then spread to the field. My dad was a fireman so he had to go and my mum was still at work, which meant I had to stay home and look after my little sister. So, I didn't go to the pond. Hayley was disappointed but she went along with her best friend, Deborah. That's what she said she was going to do. And that was it. No one ever saw those two again. They vanished.

"Of course the police searched the whole area as well as the pond. They sent divers in but there was never any trace. No one knew what had happened. Stunned the village, I can tell you, and though it's been twenty five years I don't think people would want any of those old memories stirred up again, just in case the villagers get a bit sniffy about what you're doing. They can be a funny lot."

Dr Helena Judd clicked her recorder off. "Thank you very much Mr Enerson. I appreciate you telling me about such a sad event."

"Call me David," he said sitting back and feeling strange to have recounted the story. He hadn't spoken of it for years, maybe ever. He watched the young woman putting away her notebook. He thought how odd it sounded when people referred to him as Mr Enerson. It only happened when he was called into the conservation offices for official nonsense – like this.

"Everyone in my department is very grateful to Lindesege District Council for allowing access to the area," Dr Judd went on, smiling softly. "And of course for lending your expertise as well, David."

He snorted. "I didn't get much choice in the matter." He realised it sounded unfriendly and checked himself. "I mean, it's not often our local university has these sorts of research projects, not round here anyway."

Dr Judd nodded. "You're right. As an institution I think Lindesege University often forgets what is right under its nose, but not my department and not me. This area is perhaps the most unique and unexamined in the whole of northern Europe. It's a great opportunity."

"What did you say was the name of your department?"

The young woman closed her satchel. "We're part of the archaeology faculty but this project incorporates our folklore and mythology departments working more closely. It's a new venture and could open up many funding streams." She bit her lip. "If I'm successful," she added.

"Sounds like a lot of work," David surmised.

"It will be. Right now I'm making preliminary notes with a view to returning in the summer for a more thorough investigation. Then I shall have a small team with me."

"I see." Typical, David thought. Once again the council hadn't bothered to inform their sole conservation officer of any of the finer details of this joint venture. Their primary concern seemed to be funding and publicity rather than the plight of water voles or the whirly gig beetle, both of whose populations were threatened by habitat fragmentation, pollution and now university students clomping about.

"We will be as careful as we can not to disturb the wildlife," Dr Judd reassured him, reading the miffed expression on his face.

A little embarrassed, David looked at his watch. "You wanted to see the stone circle and then the pond didn't you?"

"Yes please," she smiled. "If there's time."

As they drove past Scaraby Woods in David's Land Rover, Helena Judd told him more about her excitement for the project. He thought it sounded like a lot of nonsense but he admired her enthusiasm. Who was he to judge, he reflected. Most people thought his excitement about rare species found in Lincolnshire's chalk streams was dull nonsense. As she spoke he understood that she saw something very different in the land about Low Scaraby. For her there was mystery, whereas for him there was simply a fragile ecosystem. At the Crow Hill stone circle he parked and they walked to the centre of the stones.

"You see these stones date back further than those of Stonehenge; perhaps as old as 3000BC," Helena told him. "There are markings and carvings on them which have no correlation to any other glyphs ever seen. They are quite unique. Extraordinary even. This place has a dark past. No one knows for certain but it could well have involved ritual sacrifice."

David wondered if that was why he always felt out of sorts whenever he went up there. Buzzards too always seemed to circle mistrustfully above the stones and foxes, he had noticed, went around the site, never through it.

"We think in the late Neolithic period there were many more ponds scattered in this area," Helena went on. "The Nether Pond is perhaps the oldest and largest one remaining. It is likely there is an underground stream that runs from this hill and down into Nether Pond."

"You mean that Nether Pond is connected with this place?" David felt dispirited. In the same way he disliked the stone circle, conversely, he enjoyed Nether Pond. Aside from the tragedy that one summer it was a place of tranquillity, brimming with all manner of creatures and wildlife. It was the sort of place that made his job seem important. Crucial.

"Our theory is that tribes in this area held a unique set of beliefs, ones that centred on water deities. We think that rituals were held here and then sacrificial objects were taken to nearby ponds as offerings."

"Human sacrifice you mean?"

"Possibly, though it could often be artefacts as well, like pottery and jewellery. Look." She opened her satchel and rummaged inside, her dark auburn hair scattering across her features from the breeze that forever twisted about the stones. "Here." She handed him a small metallic object, flat like a medal.

"That's very nice," David said, not knowing what he should be making of it. "Was that found round here then?"

"No," she smiled. "It was taken from a cast made on one of these stones back in the fifties. The symbol is the most common on all of the monoliths. It appears about twenty three times."

David nodded dumbly and looked at it again. To his eyes it looked like one of those washing machine instructions he never understood. There was certainly something odd but familiar about it. Then it struck him. Perhaps it was because he had recounted what had happened to his girlfriend on that summer day, but he suddenly remembered Hayley had found a small medallion that looked similar. It had been near the pond. She had found it a few days before she disappeared and decided to attach it to the silver chain around her neck. He'd almost forgotten about it. He wondered if he should mention it now but feared he might look foolish again. A serious look had fallen across his features which seemed to prompt Helena to laugh. David felt embarrassed and handed the thing back, not wanting to be reminded of the past any more that day and not wanting to explain further.

"It has runic elements to it," Helena continued, "but nothing we can pinpoint. The only corollary are elements of Egyptian glyphs linked with Nile water gods, but even that is pretty outlandish as a theory. Please don't tell any other archaeologists I just said that or my career is over."

"No, I won't," he said, suddenly concerned for her.

"That was a joke," she said touching his arm.

"Yes." David felt awkward and checked the time. "We should probably think about heading to the pond. The light will be fading soon."

"Right-oh." Helena took her camera out. "Just let me get a couple of quick photos."

"If you like." David began walking from the circle, leaving the archaeologist to it. He felt more uneasy than usual among the stones. He wondered if it was simply the presence of Helena Judd. He was more used to the company of badgers and water voles and had accepted he was hopeless with women a long time before. She was pretty, intelligent and bubbly – a dangerous combination to a man who had tried to ignore the confusing eco-systems of relationships. But it wasn't just that. The stones seemed particularly malevolent then; like he was being watched by some invisible presence. David didn't know how to explain the feeling, yet whatever the thing was, it was evil or rotten in some way. He felt it in his blood.

In a few minutes they were driving toward the pond. "There's never really been a thorough archaeological investigation of it," Helena told him. "We're hoping to link the stones with the pond more clearly and discover more about the belief systems that made them significant." She looked about at the gentle hills that Low Scaraby huddled in. "This road is actually part of an ancient track that connected the stones with the pond."

“I see.” David considered inviting the archaeologist to have dinner with him but remembered his cottage was an untidy mess. By the way she seemed to throw everything into her bag he wondered if things like that would bother her.

They parked a short distance from the pond and walked along the footpath which led to it. Usually, David felt his cares subside whenever he drew close to Nether Pond but not this time. Now he felt a vague anxiety somewhere in his gut, just like he felt at the stones. He noted there was no bird song. The trees were quiet, their hushing leaves somehow mournful to his ear.

“Tell me,” Helena said, stopping and looking at David. “Was there anything unusual or different back at the stone circle just now?”

Apart from a pretty woman who kept smiling at me, he thought. “I don’t know? I always get an odd feeling up there. I only ever go up to the stones if I have to. Why do you ask?”

"Nothing," she said. "I just got this funny feeling. I'm probably just anxious about all there is to do for this project. It's important for me that it all goes smoothly."

David was about to tell her that it would be fine and that he would help do whatever he could, but Helena realised she'd left her camera in his Land Rover. "I'll go back and get it for you," he told her. "If you carry on down this track you'll see the pond just past the bend. I'll be back in a minute." He nodded with a smile and hurried away.

When he got back to where they had parked he simply grabbed her bag and slung it over his shoulder. As he started back toward the pond he began rehearsing what he might say; casual,
indifferent almost, but friendly; friendlier than he had been back at the conservation offices. He would ask her to dinner, maybe with the suggestion that they could go over a few maps of Low Scaraby. David actually enjoyed poring over maps. He guessed that it

was probably the sort of thing that Helena might enjoy too. Then it would all seem innocent and practical. David smiled at his course of action.

His daydream died when a scream like a blade cut the evening air. It came from the pond. David responded automatically, charging like a spaniel down the track toward the water. Another scream. It wasn't a cry from being startled by something, it was a genuine howl of terror.

When David reached Nether Pond he was rooted to the spot by utter confusion. His inner voice told him what he was seeing was not real. "Fucking hell!" his outer voice responded.

A few feet from the bank, stood in the water, was some kind of beast or alien or monster. David didn't know what. It had the form of a human but must have been around ten feet tall. Its entire body looked to be made from slime covered water weeds and moss. Nevertheless, it was a recognisably human form and certainly with great strength. It held its arms out like the pose of Vitruvian man and David saw there were hundreds of feather like fronds hanging from its myrtle skin. The fronds appeared to be wafting in the air but David realised it wasn't from the breeze. The beast itself was directing them and they were pointed toward the collapsed body of Helena Judd. It wasn't just the fronds, there were tentacles too; fearsome things a deep red in colour. What horrified David most of all was where these tentacles emanated from. The beast did not have a recognisably human head. The only thing that David could think was that it looked like a jellyfish. There were no features, no eyes, just a luminescent bell that glowed like a light bulb. Where it met the shoulders there were dozens of red, quivering tentacles all reaching toward the archaeologist.

Helena's body responded by starting to rise several inches from the grassy bank where she lay unconscious. She hung limp, gradually climbing higher until several feet from the ground. The beast seemed pleased and let out a wild cry like that of a rutting stag.

"You bastard," David mumbled when he realised what was happening. The beast meant to take Helena, drag her toward its eager tentacles, then disappear beneath the water. An image of his first girlfriend, Hayley, flashed before his eyes. He understood this is what must have happened to her and her friend all those years ago. Now it was about to happen once again. Whatever the thing in the water was, beast or god, it had some kind of power and it was drawing the unconscious archaeologist closer. "Bastard!" David said again but this time loud and angry. He charged toward the pond, not knowing what he was going to do, only knowing he had to stop the thing.

The beast was startled, suddenly aware of another's presence. This new other smelt wrong to it, meant it harm, instinctively it knew. Helena's body was released and dropped into the water. The tentacles of the monster turned their attention to the conservation officer.

David felt two moist and pulsating appendages grab him by the throat and lift him into the air. He reached his hands to try and grapple with the thick, red tentacles but their slime wouldn't allow him a grip. The jellyfish head seemed to consider the thing it held then dismissed it. David was launched over the pond, landing in a large patch of nettles and reeds further along the bank.

The cool water had revived Helena and she began to swim. When she saw David land and disappear in the greenery she made straight for him. She dared not look behind her – she didn't need to. Helena could hear the beast bellowing, more aroused than before.

She reached the bank as David managed to shake the fuzziness from his head and drag himself up. He reached out his hand to her.

"What the hell is that thing?"

"Something ancient," Helena gasped. She pulled her body into the shallow mud and held out her arm for David to grab. "Whatever it is I think it has been here a long time."

David saw the beast begin to wade toward them, its powerful legs pushing through the water. He grabbed Helena, pulling her from the shallows. "Why has it appeared now?" The tentacles began flailing about, the jellyfish head seemed to have grown.

Helena fell on top of David. "Give me the satchel," she told him. She hurriedly rifled through it and pulled out the cast of the symbol taken from the stones. She turned and held it toward the creature.

The beast bellowed once more. Whether it saw the medallion or somehow sensed it, David could not tell, but it responded. The tentacles became engorged and fanned like a peacock's tail. "We've got to get away," he said scrambling to his feet and taking Helena with him. She didn't argue. "That medal's only made it angrier," David said lifting her to her feet.

David began to run toward a thick coppice of trees when, like a whip, a single tentacle flung itself toward him, cracking the air and striking the back of his head, knocking him down. It was the girl that the beast wanted. It was she who had inflamed the creature, she who had shown it the ancient symbol.

Helena turned to face it. The beast was out of the water. All its appendages reached for her and picked her from the ground, holding her aloft. She didn't quite believe what she was seeing. The green, leaf like skin on the body of the creature opened out, revealing a cavity filled with hundreds of tiny tongues. They all seemed to lick at once. It was clear that Helena was to be squeezed into this wet, slimy chamber and somehow devoured.

"No," she said. "You won't have me." Helena once again frantically searched in her bag. She found the folding knife she knew was inside. It was a tough, old knife that she always kept sharp; a gift from her grandfather and with deer antler grips. As she was brought closer to the beast she knew she would only have one chance. At the right moment she brought the blade down on to the bell of the jellyfish head. She rammed it through its membrane with a thrusting force that took all her strength.

The beast shuddered all down its body. The tentacles immediately released their prey and its humanoid legs staggered backward. Helena was in the dirt, the knife still in her hand. The beast staggered and screamed again and then its bulbous head exploded in a shower of red, white and black matter, scattering thick gunk across the trees and bushes.

The body, now headless, toppled back into the water and slowly sank below the surface, a terrible wheezing cry coming from its quivering wound.

"Are you ok?" David got to his feet and went over to Helena. She was still on the ground, covered in the dripping mucous, turning cold on her skin. David wiped it away from her face and they hugged each other.

Helena held David tight. "This isn't supposed to happen in archaeology," she said, trying to laugh.

"How do we explain what we've just seen?" David held her closer, his body shaking. "Because I haven't the foggiest. Bugs and beetles are the limit of my understanding."

They rested on each other for a moment. Helena looked up at him. "It's incredible," she said. "I don't think my colleagues at University are going to believe it."

"I don't think anyone will," David said wiping more of the slime from her face.

"How about we try and work it out over a cold beer and some dinner?" the archaeologist smiled. "I think that would help."

David nodded and Helena took his hand. They both stood and watched the black water of the pond gradually become still until there were only gentle ripples from the breeze.

THE HARVEST

Jed King came home in the midday heat to find his wife, Sheila, pleasuring herself with his nasal hair trimmers. He had entered the kitchen from the back door and kicked off his boots, calling her name. He heard the buzzing but at first thought it was a wasp drawn to the pots of jam that Shelia had been preparing. He looked about but the kitchen was still. Jed listened harder. The buzzing was not from any insect. He shouted for her again but there came no reply.

He grabbed a scone that had been left on the side and went through the hallway to the foot of the stairs. Punctuating the monotone buzz he could hear murmurs and tiny yelps. Jed let the scone hang out his mouth as he stood and listened, then after a moment ventured up the stairs.

He pushed the door of their room open. There she was, sprawled on the bed, her floral dress hitched around her waist and her knickers hung about one ankle. There she was, working the trimmers in and out of her vagina, the plastic guard still over the blades. Shelia had a sheen of sweat on her face. She opened her eyes as if remembering where she was, and saw her husband in the doorway with one of the scones she had baked that morning in his hand. He had brought in with him a smell of the onions he had been harvesting from the fields.

"They're my trimmers," he said.

Shelia had switched them off but they remained partway inside her. She felt the sudden stillness on her body and brushed aside a lock of her curled hair, once blonde but now greying, stuck to her forehead with perspiration.

"Yes," she told him, still panting.

Jed felt himself stirring. He began to pull off his shirt. As he approached the bed he saw Sheila open her arms for him. He smelt the August air in the room, felt the frame of the house and the bricks tethered to the warm earth, drew in Sheila's breath as they touched. As he began to kiss her open mouth he silently calculated the time left until he had to return to work and the onions in the fields.

LOST BEHIND THE RAINBOW

Slackerjack

The music blog for enquiring minds

On the night of Febuary 11th 1979, a full 666 days before John Lennon was assassinated by Mark Chapman, an obscure yet mercurial singer songwriter, Chip Chatterton, took the warm up spot for fatal wounds administered by deranged fans. Obviously far less is written about Chatterton than Lennon and Chatterton was never successful in his lifetime, however in recent years more interest is beginning to be taken in this mysterious figure who, like John Lennon, hails from the murky northwest of Britain.

Since that day in February nearly forty years ago, an underground but growing army of fans and idolaters have been desperately trying to obtain any of the originally recorded tracks made by Chip as a solo artist. Original vinyl records and even bootlegs are scarce. This is all set to change since Grafic Mushroom, a little known New York based label, announced their intention to re-issue the back catalogue of all three of Chatterton's solo albums, starting chronologically with 1972's *Lost Behind The Rainbow*.

The real story of Chip Chatterton, however, starts several years before his first hypnotic solo effort. The mythologies surrounding him are perhaps the most haunting and strange of any of the volatile musical talents more widely recognised; figures like Syd Barrett, Peter Green and Nick Drake. Chatterton can stand alongside all these more familiar names, for he too was a brilliant yet troubled and eccentric artist.

Charles Christopher Chatterton was born on May 23rd 1941 in a terrace house in Moss Side, Manchester. For the first month of his life he lived with his parents, Walter and Irene, and his older sister Edith. Tragedy struck when Chip was five weeks old and his father was killed in an air raid by the German Luftwaffe. Irene never really recovered from her husband's death and by all accounts became a nervous, jittery woman.

Sadly for the Chattertons, Death seemed determined to keep them close by his shadow. In 1950, when his sister was just 12 years old she was knocked down by a police car and killed. Chip was with her at the time and saw everything. "I had constant nightmares for months afterward," he told the reporter from an American magazine, in the only interview with Chip ever recorded. "I could see her face, covered in blood," he went on. "But she was smiling at me like everything was fine. In my dream she's always smiling and beckoning me to follow after her somewhere."

What followed was a dark time for Chip. His mother's mental state became increasingly frail and could no longer cope with her wild, angry son: simultaneously missing his father and feeling guilt over his sister. In 1954 when Chip was 13 years old he was sent to live with his Uncle on the edge of the Yorkshire moors.

It was a desolate space and one which the precocious young teen filled with his imagination and creativity. According to neighbours and friends his uncle was tough with him more often than not but also allowed him freedom to roam and gave him his first guitar. According to one friend, Pete Shaw, Chip became a proto-Heathcliff, wandering the moors, communing with nature, playing his guitar and exploring his inner world. "He stood out a mile by the time he was 16 or 17. Sometimes we'd hitchhike over to Whitby or Scarborough in the summer but it was always more difficult to pick up lifts when Chip was standing at the side of the road with his long, black hair and black boots, scowling at the tourists."

In 1959 Chip moved back to Manchester and for one term, possibly two, attended Art College. After that didn't work out he found a job at the Strangeways Brewery. As the sixties began Chip started playing in various local bands such as The Velveteers, The Brian Booth Four and The Rangers. By 1964 however he had grown tired of playing in club circuit bands for little more than beer money. He was itching to become a part of the new beat sound that was beginning to take hold; bands like The Stones and The Beatles were just starting to send the new youth movement into meltdown.

In January of 64 Chip was passing through the renowned Blue Boar services, now the Watford Gap. His then band, The Rangers, had played a gig in nearby Luton and were heading back up to Manchester. He got talking to a group of lads also in a band; The Fire House. They were booked to go in the studio the following week, they told him, to cut their first single for label Mariposa, only their drummer had quit on them. Chip was a multi-instrumentalist even at this point and could beat the drums as good as any mop top wannabe. He saw his chance and offered to join them then and there. They were charmed by him and decided to give him the chance.

Less than a week later Chip was the new man on the stool for The Fire House and their debut single, *She's a Good Girl*, had been recorded. It was a sweet song but with an edge of knowing not heard on many records from the era, all driven along by Chip's tight and emphatic rhythm. It's impossible to say how the song might have been different without the new drummer but certainly he had an immediate impact. Dave Young, bassist for The Fire House, remembers clearly. "I don't think we even saw him again until the day before the studio. We just rehearsed a few songs for an hour or two but it soon turned into a bit of a party. The morning of the recording we were all a bit worse for wear but Chip got us all going, making us laugh. It was like we'd known him for years. We all knew he was going to be great."

Indeed it was the beginning of a great time for Chip and his new bandmates. *She's a Good Girl* peaked at number 18, an unlikely hit that sent them on their way. A tour was hastily put together supporting The Searchers and PJ Proby. A follow up single was quickly written and recorded, this time crediting Chip as one of the songwriters. The jangly pop perfection of *Take Her To The Moon* gave them their second top twenty hit, peaking at number 15.

Dave Young picks up the story: "We couldn't believe how quickly things had come together for us. We used to say that Chip was our lucky charm. In the beginning we all got on and things were great. I probably knew Chip best as we always shared hotel rooms. Don't get me wrong he was a great guy but even back then there was something about him, some kind of darkness or sadness. It was like he could never really enjoy the success. I felt sorry for him really."

Like many groups of the era, their popularity was short lived. By 1969 The Fire House were pretty much forgotten; just one of many acts that looked out of step after the summer of love and the introspective psychedelic wave it ushered in. Chip had become bored as well. The band only wanted him to play the drums and although he got some writing credits it wasn't enough for such a creative and troubled man.

Tour manager Geoff Brady remembers one incident from their final American tour. "We had stopped at a desert town in Nevada at some late night gas station. It was really in the middle of nowhere. We were about to pay when the shop got held up. Two drunk Mexican bandito types came in shooting the place to bits. We were all scared to death apart from Chip. He just stood them down, refusing to give them any money, not that he had any. That was when I realised he had some kind of macabre self-destruction vibe about him. That was the beginning of the end."

Indeed the writing was on the wall. After a series of disastrous shows along the Californian coast, Chip finally called it quits. He no longer fit in with the others and his drug use had begun to get out of control. Dave Young: "He just stopped wanting to hang out with us, or couldn't. He was very withdrawn. We'd all taken acid by this point but none of us really got stuck on it, it was too much but Chip was different. I guess he was frustrated with the band and took himself off to do his thing. One time he showed me his notebooks just full of scribblings and drawings. He told me some of it was automatic writing, like something was just making the pen move through him or something. Looking back I think we could have been there for him a bit more, y'know."

Toward the end of December of 69 Chip left The Fire House. After a show in LA he simply drove away from it all. His car was found abandoned in the desert near Joshua Tree three days later.

For all intents and purposes, Chip Chatterton disappeared for nearly a year. No one really knows what happened or where he went. Rumours persist that he went down to Mexico and found some transcendence through peyote, others posit that he simply wandered around the American South West like a hobo, hopping trains and eating out of dumpsters. What is certain is that he washed up in LA around early 71, his black locks shorter, his frame thinner and his skin darker. With him too he had a group of acolytes, mostly a little younger than the now 30 year old Chip, and mostly dressed in dark clothes. Colloquially they became known as The Black Rainbow and Chip was their maharishi.

Around this time the mythology of Satanism and black magic that today surrounds Chip really took off. Manager Geoff Brady explains: "His mother had died. She'd been in an institution for a while. Somehow we got word to Chip out in LA but he couldn't attend the funeral. Instead I received a package with explicit instructions that I was to take it with me to the funeral and sit it next to me in the church. The package contained a simple ebony box. When I opened it I couldn't believe it. In a coffin shaped space there was a foreskin surrounded by all these weird carved symbols. Just creepy. I guessed it had belonged to Chip, if you know what I mean. To tell you the truth it scared the crap out of me. I did as he asked, I figured I owed him that much. Then I just hid it away in my garage."

About six months ago several items once owned by Geoff Brady went up at auction. As part of my research and investigation into the life of Chip Chatterton I will confess here that I bought the legendary prepuce and can confirm it's a ghoulish object that now resembles a piece of bacon moulded from candle wax.

In 72 Chip and his Black Rainbow followers finally got into a studio. There was an outpouring of songs. Years of stifled creativity and mental health issues combined and exploded to form the profoundly beautiful, confusing and tortured sound that became *Lost Behind The Rainbow.*

"It sounds like a man who has fallen through a hole in the earth and come out the other side mumbling prophecies and visions," says Niven Escobar, former hanger-on and Black Rainbow wannabe. "Chip was just pointing in another direction to everyone else and no one could figure out what direction that was. He was a genius."

When *Lost Behind The Rainbow* was released on Capitol subsidiary Algonada it could have and should have been a hit, or at least a game changer. Sadly it wasn't to be. Just three months later Pink Floyd released their seminal *Dark Side of the Moon* on Capitol. With its iconic spectrum album art, suggesting a rainbow, and related label heritage, most people assumed Chip's album was the cash in imitation. Chip Chatterton was unknown as a solo artist and The Fire House had faded from people's memories. Chip's solo masterwork quickly and quietly disappeared, even with the odd favourable review behind it. “No one knew how to market him,” reflects Bob Elbridge, executive at Algonada. “Chip himself didn’t seem to care too much so in the end it was a real car crash for everyone. Even afterward a lot of us had high expectations for his next album.”

That next album was 1974’s *Dirt of Time*. Again it was a howling cacophony from a fragile mind, in equal parts tender and hypnotic whilst gloomy and feral. Once more the label found it hard to find a place for a maverick talent like Chip and the music buying public once more neglected to show any real interest. *Dirt of Time* was the last album that Chatterton would make on US soil.

The last three years of his life again tend to disappear into dark mists of his own creation. Little is known and even less understood. We can be certain that he left Los Angeles and his Black Rainbow followers behind. We know also that he had met someone; Shanice Donelson, seven years his junior.

She'd had a troubled youth in the Midwest and by the time Chip met her she was already into magic. It was Shanice who introduced Chip to such figures as Aleister Crowley and Austin Osman Spare and the possibilities of magical workings. They were married in New York in what Shanice described at the time as a pagan ceremony. By 1976 Chip had taken his wife back to the UK, setting up home in a cottage just outside the fishing port of Whitby, famous for its association with Stoker's Dracula and close to his beloved moors. It wasn't long before their daughter Selene was born. They kept themselves to themselves, in fact most people stayed away; things were just a little too odd.

"The last time I saw Chip was a year or two before he died," Dave Young explains. "He asked me to lay down bass tracks on some songs he was working on. He was more than capable himself and I got the feeling he just wanted to see me, see someone from his past. When I got there, immediately I sensed a bad atmosphere. The place was in darkness, even in the daytime. Shanice told me she was going in and out of trances all the time, communicating with the dead or something. Chip seemed so distant and alone. I don't know. Afterward I thought it was like he knew death was just over his shoulder. I stayed one night and got the hell out of there. I never saw him again."

For whatever reason things deteriorated between the couple. Shanice too eventually left and went back to the states. She would die in a car crash in 1981. Chip and his baby daughter were ostensibly alone together.

In 1977 Chip released the final suite of songs he ever recorded: *Crux*. For the most part written and committed to tape entirely at his Whitby cottage, the album is a short, spare acoustic offering from a man who sounds like he knows the game is nearly up. Yet again the album was ignored, this time in a climate of aggressive punk and new wave sounds. One track features a collaboration with his daughter Selene. She can be heard making gurgling noises in the background and calling for her dada.

What little money he had was running out by late 78 and when invited to perform at what could loosely be described as a 'pagan festival,' he had little choice but to accept.

The venue for the mysterious gathering was on the Island of Doumon, a tiny green dot of land on the edge of the Bristol Channel, seven miles from the North Devon coast. Chip left Selene with neighbours and made the long journey south. There were reportedly two hundred people attending the event and staying on the island that weekend in the remains of derelict farm buildings.

Norman Nixon, a now former white magician, was one of the revellers. "Everything went pretty well on the first two days, even though the February weather was still pretty bad. We lit big fires and most people were there to have a good time but of course there were a few there to practice magical workings. I saw Chip perform and he was mesmerising. Then on the Saturday night the mood seemed to change; it got a lot darker. People were saying certain spirits had been called forth, dangerous elementals. It changed the entire vibe."

In the small hours of Sunday February 11th Chip was reportedly in the company of several ladies. When he got up to relieve himself, in the darkness he heard a man call his name. Moments later the unknown assassin stabbed him three times in the back. Chip Chatterton was dead within minutes.

Perhaps it is no great surprise that the murderer was never apprehended, given the remote location, lack of any actual witnesses, reticence of the attendees to talk to the police, limited forensic capabilities and the overall disinterest from the authorities to pursue a case where one freaked out hippy turned on another. Few motives were forthcoming other than drug crazed lunacy. Of course rumours soon began. It wasn't drugs, it was dark forces from another realm, taking back what had always belonged to them. Thus ended the brief, fragile life of one of the most enigmatic and exceptional artists this country has ever produced.

Selene Chatterton will be a little older now than her father when he died. Shortly after the events at Doumon Island she was sent to live with relatives from her mother's side, somewhere in the United States. Who knows if she remembers her father or even if she has heard the music he made. I hope she has. And I hope you hear it too.

Grayson Lowe

Lost Behind The rainbow is released on March 23rd through Grafic Mushroom

LAST NIGHT AT THE RED KITTEN

The grains of snow looked like glitter when wind lifted them from the top of the supermarket roof, then swirled the delicate crystals across the eerie glow of the Bigsave sign. On some other night, in some other place, Sasha would have thought it was pretty in a bleak sort of way, but not now.

Now she couldn't feel her feet and couldn't feel her backside resting on the snake of Bigsave trolleys. They were all huddling together for warmth – the silver carts and her – inside the small, plastic covered shelter, but it did no good. There was no warmth, only the cold, January night.

As a way of trying to keep calm and forget the temperature, Sasha went through each distinct step that had led her to the deserted Bigsave carpark at three in the morning, waiting for her boyfriend, Clinton Dowd, to reappear in his rusted old car:

1. Clinton waking her just after midnight, telling her to throw some clothes on and not to ask questions. The only questions she had then were *why is the light on?* And *can I go back to sleep?*

2. Clinton driving through the frosty darkness, his hands tapping furiously on the wheel, talking and talking but not saying anything until she told him to shut up, to calm down and to explain it all from the beginning.

3. Clinton leaving her in this carpark on the edge of nowhere while he went to meet a man of god. Sasha would be safer waiting there, he had told her. He wouldn't be long,

he said before throwing the car into gear and wheel spinning on the thin covering of snow.

Clinton Dowd appeared a little dim-witted to most but in the time they had been together, Sasha had come to realise, though he was guilty of many things, he wasn't stupid. She trusted him and believed his story – even though it seemed fanciful. Sasha gave a shiver and muttered a forfucksake and checked the time on the watch Clint had bought her for Christmas. She desperately wanted the headlights of his car to appear and cut through the dark and the snow and her unease.

"Good evening."

She had not heard anyone approach and looked up, startled. She saw a thin man in a camel duffle coat with its hood up. Her first thought was how warm the coat must have been, but then a deeper part of her mind kicked in and a jolt of anxiety went through her body like a camera flash going off.

"Who are you?" she asked.

The figure delicately pulled the hood back and revealed himself to be quite ordinary looking, like a school teacher Sasha thought. She would have put him at around fifty though he could have been younger; it was hard to tell in the reddish glow from the supermarket sign. Underneath the duffle coat he wore a dark grey shirt and a green tie. His trousers were black and ended about an inch too short, which made his sharply pointed boots even more noticeable.

"Your name is Sasha, is it not?" His tone indicated the question was a mere formality.

The cold she felt had gone. Sweat now gathered at the small of her back.

"You are expecting Clinton," the man gave a faint smile. His voice was matter of fact but his eyes had a look of enjoyment.

Sasha moved away from the trolley shelter. "I asked who you are. What's happened to Clint?"

"Cutter is the name I often go by."

"Cutter?" she repeated, not liking the sound of it. She couldn't remember Clint ever talking about anyone with the name.

"And as for Clinton," he went on, "nothing has happened to him."

"What do you want?"

"It is the medallion. That is the reason I am here. I've been sent by its owner. Of course, you have no idea to whom it truly belongs."

"Your mum?"

Cutter smiled at the jibe. "Although, as I'm sure you do know, it was in the possession of a certain Mr Raymond Carlisle, he did not, however, own it. You are familiar with Carlisle?" He took a couple of steps closer to Sasha, his boots making a dull crunch on the icy tarmac. "After all, he owns the bar where you work. The Red Kitten, isn't it?"

"And you're talking to me because?"

"Because of the medallion that Clinton Dowd has taken from Carlisle."

Sasha thrust her hands into the pockets of her biker jacket, trying to seem unconcerned. "I heard Carlisle gave it to Clint. Maybe you got your facts wrong Mr Cutter."

"As I said, the medallion did not really belong to Carlisle. It belonged to my superior. And my superior wants it back."

"I don't know anything about it," Sasha shrugged.

"Perhaps." Cutter was in front of her and took his hands from the pockets of his coat. His fingers were long and slender and the nails were painted black. Sasha couldn't help but gaze at their sheen. "I think you know enough," he said without taking his eyes from her.

Sasha only knew what Clint had told her as they drove to this godforsaken place, the medallion wrapped about a McDonald's bag and stuffed in the bottom of his holdall. As they sped through the night she demanded to know what the fuck had happened. Eventually he calmed down and told her.

The Red Kitten was a haggard, side-street strip club straight out of a teenage wet dream, full of dark corners and pink neon and with dressing rooms that had the perpetual fragrance of stale beer and mould masked by too much sweet perfume.

This was the place, eighteen months before, that Clinton first met Sasha. She didn't dance and she didn't strip but she knew her way around a bar and made the best Bloody Mary that Raymond Carlisle had ever tasted. When she arrived at the Kitten, Clinton held the position of manager but was really a fetch and carry man for Carlisle. Their boss was considered the big villain in the city.

At the end of a slow Monday night Raymond Carlisle told Clint to join him for a drink in his office. He was sat behind his large oak desk when Clinton got there. Carlisle poured out two tumblers of scotch and tipped one down his throat, immediately pouring another.

Clinton sensed something was amiss.

Raymond stared into nothing for a moment, while his hand fiddled absently at the medallion around his neck. Clint had never seen him without it. Now, in the dimmed light of the office, the medallion looked different somehow. Bigger maybe. Its gold hue darker perhaps.

"The noose is tightening," Raymond said, pushing his glass away after draining it for the second time.

"Mr Carlisle?" Clint had not seen him this way before. The young man gazed at the older, overweight baron sat in front of him and tried to determine the issue. Tiredness, Clint decided. More than anything Raymond Carlisle looked tired.

The older man sucked a heavy breath through his nostrils. "Take your skills and your talents and that pretty girl of yours and go and find something better than this life." He looked about him. "It's too savage."

"Is everything ok?" Clint wondered if his boss had received bad news, but if he had then why wasn't he with some of his other associates – like Terry Norton or Frank Billson?

Raymond looked at his watch as if not hearing Clint's question, then with a faint smile he unhooked the timepiece from his wrist and tossed it onto the green blotter in front of him. It made a heavy jangling sound as it landed.

"I want you to do that Clinton. I want you to do that for me," he said looking into Clinton's confused face. "After tonight I don't want you to have anything to do with this place or any of my businesses. You and your girl. You understand me?"

He didn't but nodded anyway.

"There's one last thing I want you to do."

Clinton started to speak, to say he didn't know what his boss was talking about, but Carlisle held up a hand and told him to shut the fuck up.

"This medallion," he said, taking it from his neck, "This is the thing I owe my fortune to. There isn't time to tell you exactly why and how. Many years ago I made a deal and this thing," he set the gold lump down next to his watch. "This thing is the tag I've had to wear."

"I don't follow you Ray?" Clinton was beginning to wonder if he should call someone – like Billson, or maybe a doctor."

"You just have to listen," Carlisle told him. "You just have to sit there and do what I'm asking you to do. You're a good lad. I can see it in you – so you do this and I'll make sure you're ok. You and Sasha will both be ok. You understand?"

Again, Clinton knew the best thing to do was nod.

Raymond Carlisle told him about a small village, out in the middle of nowhere, called Low Scaraby. In the village was an old, old church called Saint Bosco's. That was where Raymond's brother, John, was the vicar of the parish. Carlisle stuffed the medallion into Clinton's hand and told him to take it to his brother. "He will be expecting you," Carlisle assured him. "Take it to John; he will know what is to be done. You must go tonight. There will be others who want to reclaim this black thing. They will start hunting for it immediately."

Clinton felt the weight of it. He felt the blackness that his boss spoke of. It was like Carlisle had dropped a rotting apple into his hand.

"But what about you?" Clinton asked, suddenly afraid for both of them.

Raymond Carlisle simply shook his head. "I have been foolish," he told him. "Very foolish." His eyes grew wide, as if someone had entered the room from behind Clinton. Carlisle gave out a stifled growl as his head fell forward to his desk and he died.

For a moment Clinton didn't quite understand what had happened. He checked for a pulse but there was none. He pulled his fingers away from Carlisle's neck when he felt how cold his body had become in only a minute. Clinton didn't know much about death but he knew bodies weren't supposed to lose their temperature so quickly, like an air conditioner had been switched on. Clinton felt a wave of panic and confusion hit him. He took the medallion and climbed out the window, on to the fire escape and down the steps. As he drove back to the flat where Sasha was sleeping he kept checking his mirrors, wondering if he was already being pursued. Who it would be, he had no idea – only he knew that Raymond Carlisle had many enemies across the city.

Cutter continued to fix Sasha with his eyes. To Sasha they seemed as dark and cold as the January morning sky above her. "Clinton Dowd has taken something which he has no rightful claim upon," Cutter said. "There are precepts which must now be followed."

"I don't understand," Sasha murmured.

Cutter only waited with a smile.

Her phone pinged. She took the glowing device from her pocket. It was a video message. The footage was dark but Sasha could see it was the inside of a church. There was a stone floor and the murky shadows cast upon it from the rows of pews. The camera tracked along the aisle, the light source getting stronger as it approached the altar. The movement stopped and the camera began to zoom in. Candles had been lit, many of them. There were two men, tied together back to back in the chancel, just before the altar where Sasha could see the medallion had been placed. The camera began to move toward the figures, slumped upon the floor. First Sasha was confronted by the face of a man she did not know, only she could tell it was the vicar from the collar he wore. He had been beaten, his face bloody and both eyes swollen. As he breathed, flecks of blood spotted against the lens. The image moved about to the other figure. It was Clint. He too had been beaten, several of his teeth now missing. "I'm sorry," he lisped into the camera. "Sasha, I'm sorry." The screen went black.

Tears began to form in Sasha's eyes.

"It is not yet too late for him," Cutter told her.

Sasha wiped at her face. "But you have the medallion. If that's what matters just let Clint go."

"I'm sorry to say it cannot be that simple. When someone takes my master's amulet without just right there is a price to be paid. It is a rule we are governed by."

"But it's all a misunderstanding," she replied, stepping back and feeling the cold trollies against her. "It's all the fault of Carlisle."

Cutter took a step toward her and produced a pack of playing cards from his coat. They looked old and well used. "Misunderstanding or not," he said flicking the deck, "it has come to this and now you must do as I tell you if you wish your boyfriend to live."

"What's so special about that stupid fucking medallion?"

Grinning, Cutter flicked the cards again. "It dates back to an ancient time when there existed, what is often referred to as, the old religion. The spirits of the Earth were simple then. In those times there was only love, death and fear. Practice of the religion gave dominion over all men and women; for all felt the sun, which is love, and all walked the earth, which is death, and all felt the rain on their skin, which is fear." Cutter paused and fanned the cards in his hand. "Do you wish to save Clinton?"

She nodded.

“We will play a simple game,” he told her. “There are no tricks. We shall play honestly, and play we must. If I win the game then Clinton’s spirit is forfeited to my master.”

“No!” she interrupted.

“You shall not see Clinton Dowd again,” he went on, ignoring her protest. “However, if you should win then Clinton will not be harmed, at least no more, and he shall be returned to you here. After that, you will never see me again.”

“But you will cheat!” Her voice was shaking. “You will cheat and I will lose!”

“I assure you that cheating is not permitted. I am unable to cheat. Any dominion I have over the forces of this world do not encompass that of chance or fate. Success or failure is as likely to us both.”

“And there is no other way?”

Cutter shook his head.

Sasha breathed deeply and tried to regain some composure. She pushed the image of Clint's beaten face from her mind and told herself she would see him again and she would care for him. "What must I do?"

"It is a simple splitting of the cards. The highest card wins." Cutter shuffled the deck through his hands and gave the entire pack a final flick. "Aces are high," he added. "I shall go first."

Sasha watched as he held the cards out before him, balanced on his slender palm. With his other hand he grabbed at the deck and pulled the stack apart, holding up the card where he had split them.

"Nine of clubs," Sasha told him.

Cutter looked at the card and nodded as he passed the deck to her. "Now you," he said. "Shuffle first."

The cards were warm in her cold hands and she tried to mix them as smoothly as Cutter but dropped some on the icy tarmac. Finally she shuffled and the neat deck rested on her palm as she held it out, just as he had.

"A nine to beat," he reminded her.

She nodded. For a moment she dared not do anything. Cutter did not look at the deck. He looked at her. She closed her eyes, felt the cold, felt his eyes upon her. She could not stand it any longer and her other hand grabbed at the deck. Quickly she whipped away a splinter of cards and held it up for Cutter to see.

WILD

I used to love my job teaching primary; not being able to have children of my own I thought it was the closest I would get to being a parent. This made me sad for a time but eventually I pushed those feelings aside and found a joy in my work that for the most part satisfied me. At the year-end I could always see what huge improvements the children had made and I would wonder where the wild creatures I'd been confronted with in September had gone. This year, however, when the children stood up on the last day in our musty classroom and chorused, 'have a nice summer Miss Dorian,' I smiled sweetly and hoped never to see the little bastards again.

I'd been given them at the start of the year as the school's problem class. No one else wanted them and the leadership team flattered me into thinking I was just what they needed. From the moment 6F trotted into my classroom everything in my life began to disintegrate. It was as if they had brought a curse with them.

First, my oldest and closest friend, Sarah, revealed she had found a lump. Her decline was rapid and she had passed away by Christmas. Then, in January, I found my boyfriend of three years had been fucking his PA. He claimed I had become too withdrawn and his infidelity had just happened. After this, in April, my sister miscarried at nearly seventeen weeks. Her husband was stationed in Afghanistan at the time so it was me who was with her when the doctors removed the foetus. It was terrible, so sad and terrible.

Throughout all of this I was dealing with the class from hell; they bullied each other, physically and emotionally, day after day. Frequently there were tantrums, excrement, fights and mutilations, as well as more typical low level disruptions. By July there had been some improvement but I had become exhausted from putting on my happy face and making believe. I wanted to run away from teaching and dive into a bottle of gin.

That's more or less what I did on the first day of the holidays. I had only been in my new home for a month. After leaving my boyfriend I had rented a grotty bedsit until I found a house in a quiet neighbourhood on the other side of town from the school. There would be no danger of running into any child I might have taught. I sat in the garden with the white hot sun against an empty sky. I sank onto the sunbed with a large, cold glass of G&T in my hand and finally allowed myself to let go of the pain.

It lasted about five minutes.

The screaming and the shouting came from somewhere beyond my garden. It was hard to tell at first how near or far it was but as it went on, and it went on all afternoon, I began to realise its source was the garden directly opposite mine. I could tell nothing more because of the thickly overgrown conifers that bullied my fence and obscured the view of the mysterious yard and the house which it belonged to. At first it was the screaming children; a sound I had lived with for the last nine months. I recognised the pitch and tone. It was not the joyful screams of children playing and having fun. It was the screams of children taunting one another. The wild cries that I knew pre-empted violence.

The howling went on, then stopped when an adult voice began rebuking. Again I recognised its tone. It was a raised voice of anger, shouting the way I had spent so long shouting in my classroom. It made the ice in my drink rattle and my headache return.

The commotion continued in the same pattern. The children first, then the adult. What was being said or what it was all about I could not tell. I stared toward the dark shadows within the conifers whilst the clouds in my head continued to thicken.

Ignorant parents I surmised – just like the ones I had dealt with for 6F. "Why have so many kids," I whispered to no one, "if you hate them and scream at them all the time?"

I went inside to try and escape but the screams were only muffled and came through to my living room as well. By around four in the afternoon, and after more gin, I decided to investigate. There was no way I was going to be able to live with those noises all summer.

The bottom of my garden was all shadows from the neighbour's neglected trees and brambles that pushed against the low fence. I had armed myself with a pair of secateurs and, carefully stepping over into the opposite garden, began to cut away at the arms of plants and flowers turned wild. The space was cool and thick with green darkness but I cut and tugged and pushed myself through, receiving scratches on my arms from thorns, hidden like guerrilla fighters in the jungle.

On the other side, in front of me, was the exact mirror of my own back yard and house. Exact but neglected. The lawn was the same size and the same length but the grass bent heavy and twisted from its own weight. Dotted about this meadow, like obscured gravestones, were bits of things discarded; engine parts, a plastic doll's house cracked from the sun, an old sink thrown on its side and looking like a plateau conquered by snails. From the lawn was a patio just the same as mine, only weeds grew tall between its slabs and, even from where I stood, I could see cracks peppering the concrete. What spooked me was the sun lounger; it was the same as my own, in the same spot as my own with an empty glass, like my own, sat next to it as if I had just put it down myself.

I stood with my secateurs drawn and listened. The screaming had ceased, leaving the breeze to play among the garbage and the grass. The back door, the same red colour as mine but worn and faded, stood ajar.

I began to tread a path through the grass, disturbing flies from something I was glad I couldn't see. On the patio, the lounger was for certain the exact same type as the one I had left in my back garden. I crouched down to look at the glass next to it. Again the tumbler seemed just like mine and within it were two ice cubes sat in their own melt water as if whoever had been drinking from it had gotten up just moments before. The rim of the glass was smudged with bright pink lipstick the colour of sliced ham. For a moment I felt relieved. I did not own such a ghastly shade, in fact I hardly wore make up at all beyond a little eye shadow.

Then the screams started again. Closer now, rattling my ears. A chorus of cries like animals being tortured and then a woman's voice.

"You little bastards! Squirm and scream all you want, it's the only breath of life your crippled souls will taste."

An instinct to protect kicked in and I charged for the back door. On the other side was the kitchen, set just as my own but with rotted food and plates piled upon every grimy surface. I didn't stop and went diving for the door which led to the lounge, just as the screaming began once more.

The stench hit me at first – like rotten fish guts and cabbage boiling together – but what I saw froze my nausea and turned it to terror. I stood, staring at myself. Almost myself but haggard and gaunt. The figure had my eyes or I had hers but the rest of her was grotesque. A woman, propped in a chair with her legs in stirrups that hung from the ceiling. She was not old but her skin was carved with lines and peppered with veins like a blue gauze had been placed across her face. She was not me but her eyes were mine and they looked at me as I stared at her, shifting in her chair, naked but for a blood stained gown.

"At last!" she screeched. "You have come. Don't just stand and stare you silly thing," she pulled herself up.

"Empty the tank before they come again. I'm beginning to feel them."

The woman interpreted my look of disgust for confusion.

"The tank," she told me again, nodding her head toward the floor beneath her.

The tank was large and its glass was smeared and chalky. It made me think of the tank we had at the back of the classroom, until one child had smashed it in a rage, killing all the terrapins. I could see things floating inside.

"Too late," the woman moaned. "They've come again."

Her body convulsed and strained, her toes curling into claws. From between her legs spattered a litter of pink skinned creatures covered in mucous. They plopped into the tank below and began to squeal as if boiling. As they screamed I could see their mouths and eyes were more human than animal.

"You little bastards," the woman growled, still straining. "Squirm and scream all you want, it's the only breath of life your crippled souls will taste." She looked at me. "Drown them or this will never stop. Do it!"

"I can't," I told her, unable to look away from the panicking creatures as they scratched at the edge of the glass.

"But you knew I was here," she said as if affronted. "I can't do this anymore. I'm exhausted."

I began to stumble back as her eyes, my eyes, looked so pitifully at me. "Who did this?" I demanded. "Who brought you here?"

The cries from the tank fell silent and the woman began to laugh. She raised a bony finger and pointed it at me. "You did!" she screamed.

THE GRASS DOES NOTHING BUT GROW

Even the reception module looked bored, Traylon thought. Its bank of lights blinked lethargically like it had somewhere else to be, somewhere better. Of course for humans there was somewhere 'better.' The module's green display informed Traylon, for the ninth time since he arrived, that its name was RUPERT and it was now 4.37pm, August 13th 2128. Friday.

Traylon sighed and looked about at what had become familiar surroundings for him. The yellowed wallpaper had bubbled on most of the walls and peeled in most of the corners. On the carpet were the scuff marks and grime of the many not quite happy people that had sat and waited, just like him. Traylon observed the dirt on his own boots and felt a fleeting satisfaction that he had also made his own little contribution to the shabbiness. This was now his eleventh visit.

He felt like getting a coffee before he went in but knew the machine in the hall was empty. In all his ten previous appointments it had remained empty. No one was coming to re-fill it.

RUPERT's vocal synthesizer broke the silence. "Mr Hubbard, Dr Shepherd will see you now. Go on through."

"Thanks," Traylon replied flatly. It was the first time he had spoken that day and his voice sounded odd to him.

"You're welcome," replied RUPERT in a mimesis of politeness.

Dr Shepherd's office bore the semblance of upkeep. It was always dusted and the petals of the plastic flowers on the corner table were always wiped clean. Sometimes it even looked as if the carpet had been vacuumed or at least swept. Traylon wondered if it was Dr Shepherd himself that made the effort. There were very few cleaners left and Bots were relatively expensive these days.

Shepherd had a freshly lit cigarette in his mouth and looked a little tired. He moved from behind his neat desk and held his hand out to his client. "Good afternoon Traylon." He gestured for them both to take their usual positions at two comfortable leather armchairs. They were the kind of soft, warm chairs that always made Traylon feel like nodding off. "You don't mind the cigarette smoke do you?" Shepherd brought with him Traylon's file and a small glass ashtray. "I've been in augality so much this week, I forget these things do actual harm."

"Don't you have many clients left to bring you back to old reality more often?" Traylon asked.

"A few more have made transition, plus the government have less and less work to give me now. Is it ok?" he asked once more, sitting down and tapping the end of his cigarette at the ashtray.

"I don't mind," Traylon told him. "We have begun now?"

Shepherd opened the file. "Are you anxious today Traylon?"

"Just tired."

There was silence while Dr Shepherd flicked over his previous notes. Traylon no longer worried about everything he told his therapist. "I've been cutting grass all morning," he explained. "It gets hot in the solar fields."

"Of course," the doctor smiled warmly. "You maintain the solar panels. Without those there would not be enough energy for augmented reality itself. A valuable job."

"It's a job," Traylon confirmed.

Shepherd stubbed his half smoked cigarette out. Traylon took it as a sign they were now getting down to business and took note of the time by the clock that hung behind Dr Shepherd.

"So how have you been feeling this week?" In Shepherd's hand was now a pen.

"Same as last week I suppose." Traylon made a show of thinking about his answer although he didn't need to. "I've just been getting on with things. Work's been busy. Grass does nothing but grow this time of year."

"Hmm," the doctor replied thoughtfully. "Have you done your homework? How long have you spent in augality this week?"

"About two hours."

"And what did you do?"

"I went to a library and I went to a swimming pool."

"Indoor or outdoor?"

"Does it matter?"

"Just answer the question Traylon." Dr Shepherd tried to sound genial but found it harder to regulate emotions in oldality. In augality feelings were almost manufactured for you, or at least the ones you had were manipulated.

"Outdoor."

"Good, that's good."

Traylon failed to see any difference. "But I just started to feel sick again," he went on. "Especially in the library."

Shepherd wrote something in the file then looked back up at his client. "Tell me again about the feelings you experience in augmented reality – when you begin to feel anxious."

Traylon breathed wearily. He had described it so many times. Sometimes he wondered if Shepherd did nothing more than draw silly pictures whilst pretending to make notes, or daydreamed about being back in augality. That's all augmented reality was,

Traylon thought. One big daydream. "Well it comes over me like a wave," he began and Shepherd scribbled something down. "Feels like I can't breathe."

"Do you feel it coming on?"

"Yes, but it is very sudden."

"Do you ever feel like that in old reality?"

"Only when I'm in therapy," Traylon smiled.

"Of course." Shepherd mirrored the smile then wrote something down.

Grant Shepherd was finding it difficult to concentrate. He and his wife, Eleanor, had recently found a new dream house that had opened up; somewhere that catered specifically for couples. In their zone, vast tracts of digital space had been expanded and plenty of niche businesses had moved in. He and Eleanor certainly had time and money to explore their depraved fantasies. Within augmented reality there was much less demand for a psychiatrist. People instead had a multitude of ways to exercise their demons. Mr and Mrs Shepherd made sure they enjoyed their time and freedom in augality as a result. It was only a few awkward types, like Traylon Hubbard, who couldn't or wouldn't take the step into pure digital existence. Shepherd remembered the night before and the young couple he and Eleanor had shared, how far they had wanted to be pushed.

"What about the dream houses?" Shepherd asked Traylon absently. He refocused and pulled another cigarette from its packet.

"Haven't used them. I like the library."

"But in the dream houses they let you do anything. You could even fly."

"I don't like heights."

"Do you like being afraid of heights?"

"I like being on the ground." Traylon watched Shepherd inhale on his cigarette, letting the smoke drift between them. He sensed the doctor's frustration with him. At least, he assumed it was frustration. "Can I ask you something doc?"

"Of course Traylon. Remember, this is a conversation."

"On average, how many sessions does it require?"

"You mean before a client accepts transition to augality?"

Traylon nodded, the smoke beginning to sting his nostrils. He glanced at a small window that opened out on to the street. It was closed shut and made opaque from layers of grime both inside and out.

"There is no typical client. Some people take a few sessions, some take more."

"But how many do the government fund you for?"

"Twelve," Shepherd said. "But I can push it further in some cases," he added. "You don't have to be concerned, Traylon. The government are keen to have complete take up. By the close of the decade that dream will be a reality."

"Reality will be a dream, you mean."

"Indeed." Shepherd faked a laugh. In his mind popped the young girl from the previous evening. Her screams. At first of pleasure. The demands from her boyfriend, himself being thrashed by Mrs Shepherd. The boy had screamed at Dr Shepherd to go further and Shepherd had allowed himself to get pulled along by the frenzy. The dream house itself, its programming, seemed to push him on. His wife pushed him on.

"Dr Shepherd?" Traylon felt it had been an inordinately long pause.

Grant Shepherd shook himself. "Tell me about your parents."

"Again?"

"Please. I understand it seems repetitive but it is important."

"My mother died about five years ago."

"That's right," Shepherd said remembering and flicking back through his file. "It was in old reality wasn't it?"

"A hospice," Traylon confirmed. "It was long, slow and painful for her." He had gone over the details before in an earlier session and wasn't prepared to again.

"That's right," Shepherd repeated. The girl was there again. The veins on her hands as she gripped at her bindings in terror. "And your father?"

"He's dying now," Traylon reminded him. "Could you stub out your cigarette please?" He began to feel annoyed.

"Of course. I'm sorry." Dr Shepherd crushed the red cherry into the ashtray and felt the sting of heat on his fingertips. He remembered the cigarette burns on young skin.

"I think I told you in our last session that my father is now in augmented reality. He's dying so my sisters have arranged for him to end his days in a death house. I'm told he's very happy. He believes he's in a beautiful walled garden. He sits on a bench, watching bees on the lavender and looking at the manicured lawn that never grows too long."

"This upsets you?"

"I never got on with my father. My sisters look after him."

"And they are both in augality?"

Traylon nodded. He suddenly felt a desperate urge to be outside in the open space, back at work even, at the solar fields.

"Do you visit your sisters ever in augmented reality?"

"Sometimes. They still come back to reality to tie up business from time to time."

"You mean old reality, Traylon."

"What kind of death will my father have Dr Shepherd?" He pulled himself to the edge of the armchair.

"You mean..."

"Will he be aware? Will he suffer?"

The doctor closed the file and rested it on his lap. The girl had been excited. Thrilled. He could tell she was enjoying it, enjoying seeing her boyfriend, the arrogant prick, getting thrashed by Eleanor whilst barking orders, telling Dr Shepherd how to enter her, how to hurt her. The dream house too seeming to allow it, doping his mind with an equilibrium of pleasure and pain. Dr Shepherd was not to blame. How could it be his fault?

"Will he suffer Dr Shepherd?" Traylon asked again. "How does death work in augmented reality?"

Shepherd desperately wanted a cigarette now. "Augmented reality is like returning to the amniotic cave, the womb," he told him. "It supports us, it gives us the cushion on which our dreams and desires may float. It is the complete integration of synthetic intelligence and organic intelligence, yet it does not mean it gives us an escape from death. It can, however, blunt the sharpness of death's teeth. Perhaps for your father he will be sat in the garden, gradually evening will come on and for him it will be like falling asleep. The death house will see to all of it."

Traylon thought for a moment and nodded coolly.

"Is that what you wanted to hear?" the doctor asked.

"I do not get on with my father. He was not what you would call loving, but I do not wish him pain and suffering. That would not be right."

"Of course," Shepherd said neutrally. He opened the file back up and scribbled down 'pain and suffering.' He saw the dead girl's face, her matted hair stuck across it as if she had only been swimming in the ocean. It was when things had been stopped, when the dream house security came in and pulled the girl's boyfriend away, shouting and cursing, that Shepherd smelt the room and the heavy scents that the twisted sheets were full with. He felt sick. He looked at his wife but she only scowled at him as she wiped the sweat from between her breasts. Augality administrators would have to be informed, he was told when finally they were allowed to leave.

"So what shall I do Dr Shepherd?" Traylon was conscious of their time coming to an end, of their allotted sessions coming to an end. He was beginning to think he had been wasting his time. Maybe it was all a waste of time. He just wanted to get out of the dark, grimy office and go back out to the silently decaying streets. At least the sky was blue and the sun, the real sun, was shining.

"Traylon." Dr Shepherd checked his watch. This was his last appointment, his only appointment, of the day. He did not know what to expect when he remerged into augality; what his status would be. "Every epoch," he told his patient softly, "has a revolution in consciousness. Three hundred years ago it was the industrial revolution. It swept away old ways of thinking and perceiving the world. Then, a little over a hundred years ago, there was the digital revolution and again mankind had to re-programme his thinking or face slow extinction. Now, a new revolution is at hand, in fact has been for some time. Augmented reality is mankind's next great leap. If you are not careful, you and others like you will be left in old reality, watching it slowly crumble and fall silent. It is inevitable." Shepherd tried to smile but felt sick even as he spoke. "We will get you there," he clenched his fist, feeling his fingernails pierce his palm. "And you will live deeply and more fully."

Once back out on the street, Traylon took a moment to enjoy the warmth of the sun on his skin and study the sky. Clouds were bubbling up over to the west. He tasted the air and decided it would rain that evening.

As he drove back to the solar fields he saw no one. There were one or two dispatch Bots going about their errands but no people, not even the drunks at the cross road he passed earlier that afternoon. They had perhaps shuffled off somewhere in search of more booze.

When he got back to the depot he didn't even see Ezra. The maintenance module had already sent his partner out weed spraying to the north of Alpha field. Good old Ezra. He had four children and dozens of grandchildren all permanently in augality. They never bothered with him anymore. Ezra had told the government to go fuck themselves when they offered him the subsidized counselling. Traylon wondered if he should have done the same.

Traylon was told to finish the job he had started that morning. The grass grew so aggressively in the summer, obscuring the scaffold frames that supported the solar panels and threatening the faces of the panels themselves. It was tiring and awkward work cutting it back.

SNOW LINE

We'd spent all day skiing from Meribel and across to Courcheval; one of those days where the sky was deep ice blue and it gets so warm that you can strip back to just a top and not feel cold at all. Everyone was enjoying it so much, particularly Linda's friend, Patricia, who had lost her mother in January and who was part of the reason that Linda and our other friends had mustered together and determined that we would go skiing, even though it would be late in the season. Several of our party had said it would be fine, that they had skied into April before, and with luck there would still be rideable snow even in late March.

Granted, by midday the snow became sloppy here and there but within the Three Valleys there are always sections with a good bedding, even if somewhat icy, and the people who owned the chalet we were renting – a wealthy couple from Spain – told us of the best spots to try and they were absolutely right.

There were ten of us staying at La Belle Neige, made up of five couples. We had all been away together before in various combinations but it was the first time for three or four years that we had holidayed on mass. Linda and I took a room on the ground floor. It was the only bedroom on that floor so there was a little more privacy.

The day had been so warm and fresh. We had all skied hard and then enjoyed the après ski in a bar halfway down the mountain before gliding further down, into the mush and into our chalet. Everyone was so thrilled and exuberant that it couldn't help but infect you. That was how I felt anyway. Linda wasn't like that. We laid on the bed together for a while not saying very much, listening to the ice from our skis dripping on to the tiled floor of our boot room.

"I'm going to shower," Linda told me. "We'll be late for dinner."

"I need to shave," I said looking at the clock. "Do you think you're improving your skiing so far this week? I thought you were turning beautifully this morning."

"David," she rolled her eyes as she sat up on the edge of the bed and began pulling her leggings off. "After all these years, it will never be better. Twenty years ago, perhaps."

She stood with her back to me, naked then but for her bra. "So silly," she muttered and went into the bathroom, closing the door behind her.

We had not had any kind of intimacy since before the autumn. I couldn't even say for certain when it might have been. Christmas was a trial. Our daughters returned home and noticed something was awry. I told them I had been over-working and Linda said she was worried for her friend Patricia whose mother was very ill. They seemed to accept this, but that wasn't it. That wasn't it at all.

I stood in the warm, comfortable bedroom, alone, and slowly peeled my ski wear off into a small pile that looked like a black cat sleeping at the end of the bed. I thought of the speed of the mountainside, the hollering calls the group made as we slipped our way through fast runs with pines nothing more than a blur. Linda and I sat on the chairlifts. Forced close. I remembered our skiing holiday shortly before we were married and how passionate it had been in those days. She looked at me then like I had her spirit in a jar and didn't mind one bit.

I went into the bathroom to shave. Linda was already under the large chrome head of the shower. I saw my face in the mirror, my features blurred by a thin layer of steam. I could have been another man in that cloudy, downlight reflection. Everything could have been different. I sat on the toilet next to the sink and watched my wife showering. Watched her body turn about the water, her hands, turning and massaging along her form, turning the way she turned down the mountainside, ahead of us all, gliding along and free, cutting arcs on the edge of blades. Her eyes were closed, her face without strain in the steam and the water.

My hand was on my swollen member as I stared at her. As I stroked I felt my back fall against the cold porcelain and my toes flatten on the tiled floor. She saw me.

"Come here," I told her.

She turned the water off and continued to look at me.

"Come," I said again.

"No," she shook her head. "What are you doing?"

"Please." My hand continued to stroke. "Lets."

She grabbed a towel. "I told you, no."

"At least watch me. At least that. Please Linda."

She stood holding the towel against her, looking at me. "David, you're ridiculous." She left the bathroom without closing the door.

I remained sitting on the toilet, not moving. I sat while the bathroom got cold.

A VOICE IN THE FOG

The bony trees were flossed with mist and hovered at the roadside like phantoms. Three times a creature flew out across the windscreen as if escaping a predator hidden by the gloom. Each time Horkstow thought he would strike it with the car; first was just a pigeon, second an owl and lastly he didn't know what. A bat? Something that gave him a bad feeling. Something that ushered in the dusk proper.

"Fuck, I don't like this place. There ain't nothing but mud and shit and fucking fields. How do people actually fucking live here?"

Ted Horkstow didn't answer the boy. His name was Chase and he had been staring out the window, goggle eyed, ever since they left the grime of the city, its high rises watching them leave.

"You've never been into the countryside before?" Horkstow asked.

Chase sucked on his vape and expelled a cloud of cherry flavoured fog. "Once went to Scarborough for my nan's funeral when I was six. All I remember is getting fish and chips on the way home."

"We'll be back by dawn," Horkstow told him. He considered the next several hours stuck with the boy – if he wasn't sucking on his smoke machine, he was biting his fingernails. Ted thought he was a typical dead-eyed youth, the kind he saw scavenging their way about the city because there was little else to do. For some reason, recently appointed crime boss Frank Billson, seemed to think Chase showed promise. Horkstow hadn't seen any yet.

"Good. It's too fucking weird out here," Chase decided.

Horkstow said nothing. He was doing this as a favour to Billson. He and Frank went back a long way – for anyone else he would have told them he didn't do this kind of thing anymore and they should find another hatchet man. He couldn't say that to Frank. Frank Billson had done a lot for him. When Ted's wife died suddenly, he'd crumbled and it was Frank who took care of everything. It all happened soon after Ted had retired. Frank arranged for Horkstow's wife to be buried in a decent plot, with a decent headstone. Billson had even purchased the adjacent plot for Ted to be next to his beloved, when the time came. Ted could never have afforded it. Not without Frank's help.

Ted looked over at Chase who itched the inside of his ear with the mouthpiece of his vape. The boy extracted it, examined what had collected on its end, then shoved it in his mouth. Ted Horkstow had only agreed to this expedition with the boy because he felt obligated. He owed Frank and Frank had decided that the young man showed promise on the streets. So that was that. He would be allowed to go along.

"This your motor?" Chase asked.

"Yes."

"Only wondered if Frank had sorted it out for you. For the job."

"It's mine," Ted confirmed. "A 1983 Mercedes 300."

"Fuck. That's like, fifteen years older than me! Why don't you get a new car?"

"I'm happy with this one." His wife had always loved the car.

Chase poked the vape back in his ear. "This fucking place," he said looking out of the window again. "Can't be any fit girls or decent clubs or anything for miles." He turned to Ted. "So we're bumping off some old girlfriend of Mr Billson?"

Horkstow shook his head. "You're just here to observe. If I need your help, I'll tell you."

"But that's it, isn't it? We're killing someone?"

"Yes," Horkstow said, keeping his eyes on the foggy dusk in front of him. "That's what's going to happen."

"Mint."

Up ahead, just on the other side of a railway track that crossed the road was one of those country convenience stores that sold everything. At its front were displayed a variety of snow shovels and string sacks full of firewood. Ted turned off the road and on to the gravel forecourt.

"What we doing?" Chase wanted to know.

"Phone box." Ted nodded at a call box set back from the road a little way from the store. Ted looked about. The spot was deserted and there were no other cars. "Frank gave you a number didn't he?"

The boy ferreted inside his jacket pocket and pulled out a crumpled piece of paper. He handed it over. "Suppose the number isn't traceable to Mr Billson."

"That's the idea." Ted stopped the engine. There was silence and outside the gloom felt closer because of it.

"Well?" Chase twitched.

"First lesson. Things cannot be rushed. You have to be satisfied that everything is as it should be." Ted waited a moment. "You stay here."

"I want to get a drink."

"Don't go in there." Ted nodded toward the shop front. "I'll only be a moment."

"Fucksake." Chase took out his vape and chewed on the nozzle.

"Just wait," Frank reiterated and got out of the car.

In the telephone boxes in the city there were usually business cards for massage parlours and escort services. Inside this one there was nothing – not even a scent of piss. Ted unfolded the piece of paper and rested it on the small shelf. He lifted the receiver, dropped in his coin and dialled the number. On the third ring, Billson answered.

"Horkstow?"

"Yes."

"You at the location?"

"Nearby. About three miles from her place."

"That's good."

"So it's still on then?"

"Yes." Billson confirmed. "It's still on. Is there a problem?"

Ted looked out at the empty road and railway track turned fuzzy with the fog. "No. It's just that Elizabeth has big connections. You both go back a long way."

"You think I don't know? You think I do this lightly?"

"No."

"Things have been in flux since Carlisle died. If Elizabeth had acted with more respect this could have been avoided."

"I'm not involved with things anymore," Ted explained needlessly.

"So you are the best man for this. Elizabeth has to be removed. She's become greedy. You can still do it, Ted, can't you? Just like you used to."

"No problem Frank."

"Good."

Horkstow still wasn't sure what he was supposed to do with the boy. "What about Chase?"

"I know he's wild at the edges. He just needs learning. You got to start somewhere – he might as well learn from the best."

"This is a one off Frank. We talked about this." Ted shifted his weight inside the box and felt the revolver in his coat slap against him.

"Just make this a clean job, Ted."

"Of course."

"Call in a couple of days."

"I will."

Frank Billson grunted and hung up.

Ted stayed in the telephone box for a moment. He looked at the sign that gave its location; Low Scaraby Junction. Next to it was a poster that warned him about rural level crossings. *STAY ALERT!* It read. *YOU'RE ON DANGEROUS GROUND.* He pushed open the heavy door and walked back to the car.

Chase wasn't there. Ted muttered a curse. He took out a Dunhill and lit it. As he inhaled he tried to remember when he was the boy's age. He had been more attentive, more switched on than Chase, he was certain of that. He stood and waited. His feet got cold in his boots but he stood and fixed his face into the black look he was going to give the boy when he emerged.

He waited. Chase did not appear. After five minutes Ted grunted, stamped out his cigarette and trudged toward the shop. He went inside as quietly as possible, thinking he would sneak up on the little bastard. Inside all was silent. Ted guessed the counter was toward the back but he couldn't see it behind the two aisles stacked high with items like wellington boots, packs of toilet tissue and various buckets of different shapes and sizes. He checked both aisles in turn. No one. He walked to the back of the shop. There was no one behind the register but in the middle of the counter had been left a can of energy drink.

Ted felt the wrongness of the situation. He looked at the can, sweat beading on its surface from having been recently removed from the fridge, then he turned around and surveyed the shop. He took everything in; observed the cracked paint on the walls, the hum of the refrigerators, the grey murk outside that seemed to be pressing against the front windows. Ted didn't like any of it. As he turned back to the counter his foot slid a little. He looked down and saw blood; squirted across the linoleum like an action painting. Suddenly the blood was all he could smell, then his other foot slipped. He grabbed the edge of the counter to stop from going down.

"Bollocks," he said, knowing somehow the situation had turned bad. His eyes followed the whirls of blood making a trail across the floor toward a door marked 'Private.'

Before Ted had steeled himself to find out what was on the other side of the door, it opened. A man charged out, frantically swinging a hammer.

"Bollocks," Ted said again, stepping back, slipping in the blood and this time stumbling. The man with the hammer was swinging down on him. He too slipped and both men fell together. Ted noticed there was already blood splatter on the weapon but then he was fighting not have his own skull cracked open by the thing and everything became frantic.

"I've got him!" the man said gleefully. "You were right sir," he added. "I've got him."

Ted didn't know who the man was talking to but he was annoyed by his cocksure attitude. With his leg he managed to kick out and strike the attacker in the ribs. It soon shut him up but he didn't relinquish his grip on the hammer. Ted began reaching into his coat for the revolver. The man struck him and made contact with Ted's collarbone. Ted felt a shudder of pain. The jolt it sent through his body was enough to unbalance the man on top of him and push him back. Ted began scrambling to his feet. He was up. Then something clattered him on the side of the head. Not the hammer. Ted went down again and realised it was the can of energy drink the man had smacked him on the temple with. The strike had been enough to shear the can and he could taste its contents dripping into his mouth like sugary battery acid.

"I got him sir!" the man shouted. "I got them both for you."

Ted wanted to tell the lunatic he had made a huge mistake but the words wouldn't come. Instead, everything went fuzzy and he blacked out.

Ted opened his eyes and knew that his gun had been taken from him. He felt its lack of weight inside his coat. He'd been placed in a chair and his hands bound behind him. From the texture of the binding against his wrists he could tell it wasn't rope but more likely plastic cable tie – and not the strongest. Amateur, he thought. Whoever had done this didn't have much experience.

"You need to keep your mouth shut friend. Don't start any screaming. No one going to hear you any road." It was the man with the hammer only now the hammer had been replaced by a shotgun resting across his lap.

Ted glanced about. His skull throbbed when he did so. They were in some sort of lock up. He could smell grease and dirty metal hidden in the shadows.

"You're son is dead," the man told him. "He looked like a rat." He stood and swung the shotgun at Ted. "I've killed rats before but not as big as him."

"He's not my son." Ted wondered if Chase had a family who would care that their boy had died violently. He felt a touch of sadness run through him but it was gone in a moment and his next thought was for his own chances of survival. They were better now he was on his own. "You've made a big mistake," he told his captor.

The man grunted. "What you say and who you are don't mean nothing to me." He leant the shotgun on the chair behind him and stepped toward Ted, bending down to look him in the eye. "I did what I had to do."

The whiskers on his face were somewhere between a beard and not bothering to shave. Ted put him in his late forties. His neck was full of lines and looked the way a dry river bed might look to a bird in the sky. The man continued to stare. He held up his hand and with a crooked finger, poked at the cut on the side of Ted's forehead. Ted had seen plenty of dangerous eyes in his time. Eyes that had nothing but anger or lust or a determination to cause harm, but these eyes had something else. Ted wasn't sure what it was but knew it was bad. Some kind of desperation.

"Who were you talking to?" Ted asked. If the man expected him to flinch when he pressed at his wound then he would be disappointed. Pain had been a common occurrence for Ted back in the day – it was funny how quickly his body accepted it again, like putting on an old suit you'd never gotten round to throwing out. In fact, Ted almost enjoyed the physical hurt. It was better than the grief he'd endured after his wife died. That had been an insidious kind of suffering and he'd struggled with it. "You were talking to someone when you attacked me," Ted went on. "So where's your friend? Is he the one who tells you what to do? Maybe I should speak to him."

The man just laughed and rubbed his hand down the grubby shirt he wore, wiping the blood from his finger. "Mr Sawyer will speak when he's ready." He picked the shotgun back up and screwed his face into a frown. "You had a gun in your coat. What were you doing here?"

Ted smiled. "Me and the boy were just passing through. We weren't looking for trouble. You and Mr Sawyer have made a mistake."

"Mr Sawyer doesn't make mistakes. He knows things. He said people would try and take him away."

Ted held the man's gaze and wondered if, somehow, he could retrieve the small switch knife he kept in his boot. It would be his best chance to get free.

The man lifted the shotgun and pointed it at Ted. "Why'd you have a gun?"

"Same reason as you. Protection."

"I don't believe you. You were both coming to take Mr Sawyer away." He shoved the barrel closer to Ted's face.

Ted shook his head. "I have no idea what you're talking about. I don't know who Mr Sawyer is."

"You're a liar." His finger curled around the trigger. "You work for the government don't you? You want to take him away."

"This is just a misunderstanding." For the first time Ted flinched. He could smell the gunmetal.

The man cocked the trigger.

Ted closed his eyes.

The light bulb above them began to flicker wildly. From somewhere beyond the lock-up came a terrible moaning sound like the wind was fighting with the gutters.

The man lowered the gun and stared at the light. "It's Mr Sawyer," he said with reverence. "He wants to communicate." The distant howling continued in rhythm with the frantic bulb. The man seemed to forget Ted. He lowered the gun and scurried away. From the shadows Ted heard a metal door open then close. The lightbulb ceased its flickering and the noise stopped. Ted was alone.

He could feel the knife down in his boot, impossible to reach until he broke his hands free. With some effort he knew it could be done and he knew he had to be quick. Ted stood up from the chair. He breathed, deliberately, deeply, focusing on the breath. He took his mind away. A big pull of air into his nostrils. He thought about his wife. He saw her the way he always liked to remember her when they were together in their home. He could see the rose petals on the wallpaper where she sat. He could see the way she smiled at him. Ted took another breath and raised his arms up behind him until his coat tightened about his shoulders. He lifted his arms higher until it began to hurt but he saw the rose petals and her smile and he pulled his arms higher until they were about ready to tear his shoulders from his scapula. One more breath and he slung his arms down with everything he had, using the pain like rocket fuel. The cable tie at his wrists made a tiny clicking noise as it snapped apart. Ted took a gulp of air as his vision blurred and he fell back on to the seat. He continued to breathe, letting his arms dangle at his side, the pain draining down their length like blood from the throat of a slaughtered animal.

Before he could gather himself enough to move, his jailer returned.

As the man approached the light from the dim bulb above, Ted could see he was pushing a wheelchair. On the seat was a box, like some old fashioned radio; the kind that Ted remembered from his childhood. Unlike radios however, the box was metallic and had several blinking lights and at its front, like a single eye, was a circular screen with a faint green glow. The man stopped and turned the wheelchair so that the box faced Ted. The green eye stared.

"What the fuck is this?" Ted asked, his hands balled to fists behind him, ready to lash out when the moment was right.

The man held a finger to his lips. "Wait," he told Ted. "Mr Sawyer will speak."

The green glow from the eye became brighter. Ted realised it was some sort of oscilloscope. From the back of the box there came a howl of fuzz and static. In a moment the erratic noise began to settle, as if it had found a channel it was comfortable in. Ted felt the hair on the back of his neck standing up. Then out of the white noise there came a voice – human, but not human.

"This is one of the prowlers?"

"Yes Mr Sawyer, just like you said."

"And the other is dead? Is that correct Mr Langworth?"

The man nodded. "I wrapped him in tarp and put him in the store room."

"Is it now dark outside?"

"Yes Mr Sawyer. Dark and foggy."

"Then you must take the body and put it in your truck. Make sure you are not seen."

"You want me to do it now?"

"Yes Mr Langworth. Do it now. I wish to talk to our other prisoner."

Ted couldn't make sense of what he was seeing in front of him – something that glowed with flickering lights and had a voice from within just like a badly tuned radio.

"Mr Sawyer?" the man called Langworth reached down and touched the box with his fingers. "Do you think my mother might come to us tonight?"

The box did not answer but instead there were whistles and crackles and then the voice returned as if the signal were restored. "There is no way of knowing for certain," was the response. "Now do as I have asked. And bring your shotgun when you return."

"Yes Mr Sawyer." Langworth gave Ted a malevolent look before leaving. The metallic door shut and Ted was left with the static hum from the machine in front of him.

"Your name is Ted Horkstow," said the machine. "Is that not correct?"

"Who the hell am I talking to?"

"I need your help Mr Horkstow. Please, you no longer need to pretend that your wrists are still bound. You must relax and listen to me."

Uncertain, Ted took his hands from behind him.

"There is not much time," said the voice, metallic and cold and yet somehow more strained than before.

"What are you?" Ted asked.

"I can only explain in the briefest way," the voice replied, followed by the attendant static hum.

"Then explain."

"My name is Mr Sawyer. What you hear of me now is just the disembodied spirit of the man I was. Whatever I became after death, it is now held in the grip of this infernal machine."

Ted leaned forward in the chair and took a closer look at the thing in front of him. The casing looked battered and old, like something from the cold war. "You're a ghost? Is that what you're saying?"

"I am a spirit. That is all. I am what was once a man called William Sawyer. In life people considered me a bad man; my beliefs were dark and strange to others. When I died I was not mourned and was buried at the edge of the churchyard in the village of Low Scaraby not far from here. That was in 1947."

"You're telling me your spirit is now in this machine? How?"

"I do not know. Many years ago the electronics of this box captured me. It was done by a man named

Kessel. His machine took me from the void where I had been. This machine is the cage of my spirit. Unless it is destroyed I will never be set free. I want to return to where I came from. Back to death."

Ted tried to understand what he was being told. He thought for a moment. "What about our friend, Langworth? Why not ask him?"

"He is the one who has kept me here. For a long time this machine sat buried in the woods by Kessel. It was Langworth who found it and restored it and reawakened me. I have told him to destroy this thing but he has refused."

Ted allowed himself a smile. "You're a genie trapped inside a bottle."

"Yes."

"Why won't Langworth help you? He does everything else you ask him."

"There is not much time," Mr Sawyer said with more agitation.

"If you want my help I have to understand."

"I know things Mr Horkstow. I knew you and the young man would come here today. From this electrical spirit realm I can see things and I can communicate with others. Other spirits."

"And that's what Langworth wants." Ted began to understand.

"Mr Langworth uses me to communicate with his mother. She died two years ago."

"You contact the dead?"

"If the spirits allow. Mr Langworth has spoken with his mother several times. That is why he keeps me. I beg him to destroy this thing and he says he will do one day, but I know he won't. I understand his mind. He will never destroy my prison."

"So that's why you need me?"

"I am trapped Mr Horkstow. I cannot rest and I am powerless to do anything but suffer this. You though.

I knew you would come. You are a killer. You can free me from him and then destroy this wretched device."

Ted laughed. "You're a ghost."

"There is not much time. When Mr Langworth returns he will have his gun. If you do not agree to help me I will tell him to shoot you as soon as he comes through the door. He will do as I say. On the other hand, if you agree to help, I will say nothing and let you do your killer's work. Will you agree?"

The door rattled as Langworth undid the bolt.

Ted thought for a moment. "I will," he whispered and quickly felt inside his boot. He grabbed the knife and returned his hands behind his back.

The door opened. Langworth returned carrying his shotgun. "I have done as you asked Mr Sawyer," he said. "There is not a soul out there and the fog is thick now."

"Good," the machine crackled.

"I really hope my mother comes through tonight." Langworth walked toward the wheelchair. "I feel like she will. She knows I am waiting to talk to her again."

Ted opened the knife slowly. He closed his eyes. It had been a long time since he had killed. After leaving that part of his life behind, Ted hadn't thought about it and had never missed it. On the day that Frank Billson got in touch he'd had a bad feeling. Something in his blood told him it was wrong but there was something else, another voice, one that said he had nothing to lose, not now his children were grown and his wife had been taken from him. It's what he was – a hatchet man. He breathed deeply, feeling the knife in his hand.

Ted didn't give Langworth a chance to know what happened. The blade punctured his throat twice and blood sprayed everywhere, over the wheelchair and on to Mr Sawyer. Langworth dropped to his knees and Ted kicked the shotgun from his hands, almost surprised how easily and naturally the movements had returned to him. He saw the pain and confusion in the face of Langworth who gurgled rather than screamed. With a swift motion Ted sliced him across the throat and kicked his body to the concrete floor where a dark mirror of blood immediately began to form.

The whole thing lasted no more than a few seconds.

"Yes!" said the metallic voice of Mr Sawyer, louder than before. "You have done well."

Ted watched the death spasms of Langworth until his body became still. "Now he can talk with his mother all he wants," he said, beginning to feel the way he used to after a hit – like he was detached from his body, his heart only beating in the air about him.

The green oscilloscope of the box glowed and flickered. "You must carry out the remainder of your task Mr Horkstow," the voice reminded him. "Destroy the machine that has trapped me."

Ted looked from the body of Langworth to the thing on the wheelchair and folded his knife. "First I'm getting out of this place."

He grabbed the box and hefted it up. It whistled and buzzed but no voice came through. Ted felt the heat of the casing as he clutched hold of it and left the lock-up.

He stepped out and found himself in a yard behind the shop. Night had fallen and just as Langworth had said, the fog had thickened. Ted walked round the yard until he found himself back where his car was still parked. There were no lights from the shop, all was soft and dark in the damp air. He got in the car and placed the box on the seat next to him. Its lights glowed dimly with a humming noise.

"You must do it," Mr Sawyer said, now in a static whisper that was low and distant. "You must destroy this thing and let me be."

Ted ignored the voice. He thought about what it was on the seat next to him; a voice from the other side of death.

"Mr Horkstow," the voice came again, swirling and desperate. "Do as you agreed. Destroy this and send me back to the silence."

Ted thought of his wife. How he had found her body in the kitchen, collapsed in the middle of making a cup of tea. He thought of her grave and the space next to it, waiting for him. He turned the ignition of the car and switched on the headlights.

"Mr Horkstow," the voice begged.

Ted turned out of the carpark and on to the road. The car crossed back over the railway line, back the way it had come, and disappeared into the fog.

WHO KILLED SANTA?

An aroused Santa Claus is not appropriate but the man in the red suit is too consumed with rage and panic to care. His bulging member, like a smuggled yule log, is clearly throbbing from beneath the bright red Santa trousers and he's bounding down the marble white concourse of the shopping centre that's all decked out with glitzy tinsel on both its levels. Mechanical snowmen line the fake indoor street, waving him on.

Santa is running, like George Bailey returning to Bedford Falls, and his erection is bright berry red, straining against its confinement. He can't pull air into his lungs fast enough because of the synthetic rug hanging from his face. With every deep in-breath he sucks, ever more curled, grey fibres snag on his lower teeth and his nostrils become entirely clogged by the beard that's only a few polymer chains from being plastic garden furniture.

Gasps from shoppers become audible above the festive music. Some children are screaming.

An aroused Santa running through Main Street is not appropriate but what makes it worse is that he's chasing after an overweight elf who's splitting through his green lederhosen and tights, as he half runs, half lumbers away from the angry, red suited man, somehow avoiding bargain hunters dumbstruck by the scene. Elf snatches a glance behind. Santa's gained a few feet on him. When he turns back he sees that Main Street is narrowing toward the turn for the food court. Three days earlier the elf was sitting in that same food court. That's where the centre manager had decided to sit down with all the hopefuls and announce who would be this year's incarnation of Lindum Shopping Centre's old Saint Nick.

Ahead, the concourse is partially blocked by a calendar concession, in the form of a cart, parked in the middle of the street – in place since October. The elf can see multiple heads of Michael Bublè growing bigger just as Santa's hot breath grabs him from behind. A gloved fist punches him in the kidneys, a second gloved hand grapples his shoulder. Both men go barrelling into the cart, with its nostalgic barrow wheels and thirty two various dog breed calendars hanging from the eaves. Bichon Frises, tinsel, Michael Bublè, George Clooney, Santa Claus and the elf; they all go flying.

Some shoppers think it's a show. There are whoops and cheers from teenagers on the upper floor. Most people know something is wrong but they still grin at the spectacle. The younger children look the most confused at the sight of an oversized elf landing on top of Santa Claus, both men clearly in some distress.

"Mummy, what's wrong with Santa?"

"He's just excited about Christmas, darling. You shouldn't stare."

Santa is relieved to have stopped running, even though he is now trapped by the weight of the elf on top of him.

"It was you wasn't it?" Santa growls at the man above him. "You bastard!"

The elf gets hold of Santa's arms to stop them from flailing. He can feel the erection between them pushing against the exposed skin of his leg now that his green tights have ripped entirely.

"Yes it was me," the elf confesses.

"What the fuck have you done to me? My cock is hurting. I feel dizzy."

Even the elf is surprised at the stiffness of the other man's erection, beating against his thigh.

"That mulled wine you guzzled in the dressing room," the elf tells him. "I spiked it with horse Viagra. Any child that sits on your lap is going to think you're Jimmy Saville re-incarnated, at least for the next two days."

Santa gazes at the elf. His rosy red cheeks are smeared but Santa recognises the eyes staring down at him; he does not know the man but has seen him before, seen him many times. The elf was an actor, just like him.

The elf sees the recognition on Santa's face. "That's right," he laughs. "I'm just like you. I'm like the shadow that follows you, or you're the shadow that follows me." The elf had rehearsed the dialogue in his head so many times that now he couldn't quite remember what he wanted to say. "Whatever!" he spat and leaned closer, his lips almost touching the beard. "Every audition in this miserable city and you're there too."

"Am I?"

"You don't even remember!" the elf wailed. "The drain unblocker advert six months ago. The corporate video for data protection in June. Best Kept High

Street idents from April. Banquo in Macbeth. Mitch in Streetcar. Man in restaurant. Bus driver. Man in Laundrette. Undertaker. And now Santa Claus at Lindum Shopping Centre."

In a last attempt Santa tried to push the man away but failed. "You spiked my drink out of jealousy? How much did you give me?"

"Plenty."

Police were running down Main Street now. Getting closer.

"It's not my fault," Santa told the elf, beginning to see black spots. "If talent is recognised."

"Talent? Look at me!" screams the elf. "Do you see how much weight I have gained? Look how fat I am. All for this. To play Santa. I am Santa! And what happens? They pick you. But I can be an elf. A fucking elf!"

Santa says something but too faint to be heard.

"You're not special," the elf goes on. "You are just as mediocre and uninteresting as everyone else but nobody sees it because they're all too fucking stupid and in love with their own feeble ideas of what counts for fucking talent." The elf glances round at the large crowd that had gathered. "That's right!" he screams at the blank faces of the shoppers. "You're all morons. Stupid, fucking morons."

The elf turned back to Santa but Santa had gone. His eyes were closed and his body had become limp. Limp except for one part that remained indefatigably rigid. The elf could feel it even as the police pulled him away, still screaming and crying.

It wasn't until a day later when the elf got to see some of the news coverage. Whilst he was being moved to a more secure unit he and three orderlies had paused in a room with a television bolted high up in the corner. The elf was able to catch something from a rolling news channel. A reporter was stood outside the shopping centre.

"…yesterday will be a day that Christmas shoppers will not forget…" the reporter was saying. "Attempts to revive the man playing Santa Claus failed and he was pronounced dead at around 3pm. He has been named as local actor Michael Harding. Tributes have been paid to the talented man whose star was no doubt rising. His agent confirmed that Michael had recently clinched a small part in a new action blockbuster." Several pictures of Michael Harding appeared on the screen, along with amateur footage of him in a stage play. "His attacker, who has not yet been named, has been taken into police custody where he is awaiting psychiatric evaluation."

"Not yet been named?" the elf screamed. "My name is…"

But the orderlies had heard enough. One threw a blanket over his face whilst the other punched him in the gut. The third orderly had a gurney waiting to scoop him up.

On the TV the news reporter allowed a smile to appear on her face. “And now over to the weather centre for that all important weekend forecast…”

THE LAST PHONE BOX ON THE PLANET

John calls on Thursday and tells me it's bullshit when people remark *it's so hot you could fry an egg on the pavement* - at least he used to think it was bullshit but, he goes on, inside the phone box with its dusty glass, the sun is so magnified that the once stone dry blobs of chewing gum stuck everywhere are beginning to melt and drip like something satanic emerging into our world. Something satanic he says, laughing incredulously, then adds there is the faint smell of cola and pineapple.

"What about frying an egg?" I ask.

"I'll bring one with me next time," he says. I can hear the squeaking of the door as he keeps pushing it to let the heat escape.

It's July. Not just July but the hottest July, they are saying, for a very long time.

When John opens the door of the phone box I can hear the noises of the seaside. There is the faint cry of seagulls.

"My balls need some air," he tells me. "What's the time?"

I look at my watch. "Nearly two."

"I got to go."

"Ok," I say, "but you didn't tell me the new idea you had for that story."

John belches. "Yeah, next time."

He hangs up. I hear my wife calling me from the kitchen. She's eight and a half months pregnant and I'm on high alert. I think the heat could bring the labour on at any time. I think again of the softening wads of gum in the phone box.

John and I are connected by that phone box. I know it well; it is brushed steel, it is bulky, it is battered and sits at the end of the esplanade, near a carpark, a short walk from the beach.

Twenty years ago we both arrived at the town of Brightlea on Sea. We had gone there for summer work. I had just finished university and John had drifted in from some other place. I think he had been travelling around Europe until whatever money he had ran out. He was always enigmatic about where he had blown in from. We met because we had both found work in the same bar; Crusoe's. It was just a couple of streets from the seafront. After a short time we became friends and confessed to each other the exact same notion; we both wanted, somehow, to be writers.

A few days later John calls again. I answer the phone, glad it wasn't my wife. It's not that she doesn't like

John, it's more that she doesn't understand him. She doesn't understand his choices; he's remained in Brightlea, he never got married, he still writes. I gave up on the idea of making a living from being a writer and after a few years I moved away.

"It's not so hot today," he tells me, "so I didn't bring that egg."

We talk a little and then I ask him to tell me the story idea he said he was going to work on.

"Forget it," he says. "It was a rotten idea that didn't mean anything and no one would have liked anyway."

"That's a shame. I'm sure another idea will come along soon."

"I don't know," he says, and I can hear him scratching at the stubble on his cheek. "Maybe it's this weather – you know, everything so warm, everything drying out in the heat. Strikes me that everything is rotten or sour and everywhere I go I get reminded of that. It's giving me the heebie-jeebies."

This I recognise as one of his darker moods. "You ok?" I ask.

"Do you remember Stubby?" he says.

I try to think.

"He sometimes DJ'd at Crusoe's, often in the family bar but sometimes in the main bar."

"Not sure?"

"His sister was called Alice and worked in that doughnut kiosk near the pier."

I vaguely remembered him. As his name suggested he was short and he also had a mop of curly dark hair. I give John the description.

"Yes," he confirms. "That was him. The other day I was in the Golden Nugget, fixing a couple of their old machines. I went out to my van and there was a lady from the pharmacy trying to deliver some medicine. She couldn't get through the door at one of those old guest houses. They're all bedsits now. She couldn't get in and a neighbour began shouting about the awful smell that had filled the building. I went over to help. In the end we bust through the front door of this room and there was Stubby, dead in his armchair. I hadn't seen him for a long time, maybe years, but suddenly there was his corpse, in a pair of pants and a vest. He was so thin, his eyes wide open and just staring at nothing."

"That's awful."

"It was fucking sad and pathetic. This tiny, miserable bedsit, surrounded by dirty plates and clothes and porn mags. I mean, who still bothers with porn mags? Everything was so squalid and lonely. There were boxes of records too – you could tell that he had treasured his vinyl but there was a turntable with about an inch of dust on it like it hadn't been used for a very long time. The place stank of shit and death and loneliness. I came through the door and there was Stubby, sat down and looking at me like he'd been waiting for me to find him. I didn't like it. I've been walking around in a daze ever since. Imagine ending your days like that."

I told him again how terrible it must have been and no wonder he was feeling out of sorts.

"What else is there to say," he sighed. "And today I get here and there's a notice on the door explaining this phone box is being decommissioned. A couple more weeks and that's it. Gone."

Of course, John could find another phone box to call me from. You might even think it strange that he doesn't have his own phone – I agree, it is strange but that's how John is. He says it's important to keep up certain rituals. You see, when we both lived in Brightlea, we ended up sharing digs together. It was a holiday let for summer workers, so was very basic and without a phone line. Whenever we needed to make a phone call we used the same box at the end of the esplanade. It's the phone box where John learnt his first story had been accepted by a magazine. It's the phone box where I learnt I'd gotten the job in

Manchester that saw me move from Brightlea. After I moved away John remained. We stayed in touch via long letters and phone calls, always at the same phone box. It was ours the way a favourite bar or café becomes the place you always meet with friends. I lived many miles away but always ended up at that same phone box, talking with John.

"I have to go," I tell him. "I can call you later if you like."

"Nah," he says. "I'm going to see if I can write something this evening. Might be the only way out of this dreadful unease I have wandered into."

I can hear the fatigue in his voice. "Call in a couple of days then."

"Sure. How long before you become a parent now?"

"The bomb could go off any moment," I laugh.

A day or two passed. Time began to wobble like I was viewing the world across hot asphalt. I was thinking about my unborn child. I was thinking about my wife.

I was thinking about John and the corpse of Stubby. The continued heat seemed to make everything meld into one. The nights had become so warm and yet my wife had suddenly found that sleep came to her without issue. Gone was her discomfort, the constant need to pee, the struggle for her to find a position that suited. Even the heat no longer troubled her. It all seemed to fall away and once she settled at night she fell instantly asleep. I was glad for her and wondered if it was just a temporary calm before the storm of what was coming for us.

Her insomnia had not entirely vanished – it transferred itself to me instead. I began to leave her sleeping and crept about the house or stood in the garden, listening to the silence of the world at 3am. One night I was enjoying the cold kitchen tiles beneath the soles of my feet when the phone rang. I was stood right by it and answered almost immediately, almost before my mind was engaged.

"It's me," John said.

"Yeah," I said like he'd just stepped in from the next room. "My feet have cooled down. It's nice. What is it about feet? They seem to dictate how contented the rest of your body will be; they get too cold and everything is cold. Too hot and it's all too hot."

"I'm wearing flip flops," John tells me. "It's 3.18am and I'm wearing flip flops. My feet feel just right."

"Can't sleep too?" I asked.

"Guess not. This is the best time to walk around, when you can hear the hum of nothingness. Just think, in another four or five months it will be freezing cold. Everything will be stripped by the winter and this heat will be a memory more like a film you watched than something you felt."

"Let's not think about that," I told him. "I'm enjoying the sensation of my feet on the tiles. Don't spoil it."

"I told Big Frank about Stumpy," he tells me.

"Who's Big Frank?"

"One of the floor walkers at the Empire. I get called out there a lot. They have a lot of old machines and I often chat with Frank. I told him about Stumpy and how it made me feel. He said I should try meditation and yoga. Frank goes down to the beach every morning at dawn and does a twenty minute routine. He says I can join him."

I pictured John stood next to somebody called Big Frank and couldn't help but laugh. John isn't short but he is skinny. Clothes always seemed to hang from him in an awkward way and so I think people always have the impression that he is awkward in his body. He isn't. He's scruffy, certainly, but not awkward. Imagining him doing stretches and saluting the sun from the beach seemed ridiculous.

"I know," he says hearing me laugh. "I told him I'd consider it."

I tried to think of something positive to say. "You just need to get back into a rhythm with your writing." It had been eighteen months since his last book was published. It was called *Stone Below the Moon* and had come out with a small but well respected publisher. It had sold in reasonable numbers and I thought it was good – but it hadn't sold enough that he could write full time. That was why he mended old arcade machines. Since then I knew that John had been struggling to come up with something new. "It will happen," I told him. "And you'll find yourself in the groove again."

"Meditation on the beach," John repeated with a tiredness. "Meditation with Frank and medication for Stumpy; it's all the same, all the illusion of control."

I took the phone and moved from the kitchen to the sofa. "Things will be ok."

"I walked by here earlier today," John tells me, changing the subject. "There were these kids parked up in their cars with the stereos thumping. They had been to McDonalds or KFC or some awful place like that. I saw them throw their rubbish out the window. It spilled on to the grass like dog shit. I hated them so much. I could have killed them. I mean I wanted to kill them. I imagined shooting bullets at their cars or at least throwing their shit back at them, stuffing it into their faces. I didn't though. I didn't do anything."

"That's a good decision."

"Not really. I just glared while their litter danced about on the brown grass. If I see them again I swear I'll do something."

"You should forget it. It won't change anything. Try and enjoy the sunshine. Take your notebook down to the beach and write – just like we always used to."

"Think of all the phone calls made from this box, from this telephone. Think about all the lives linked to it, all the voices that have breathed into this thing, all the voices that spoke in response. Imagine all the stories that could be written out of that."

"Yes. Our voices too."

"All the breathing and the chatter, swirling through the wires, trying to express something and thirty meters away is the big old sea not giving a shit about any of it." John let out a laugh just as weary as his voice.

"Are you going to be ok?" I asked him.

"You don't need to worry about me. I was just feeling a little blue tonight but the sky is starting to get light and I think I've had an idea for a story. You just need to worry about…"

Whatever he was about to say was cut off. The line returned to its dial tone. I imagined him replacing the heavy black receiver and pushing the door of the phone box open, slouching his way out on to the esplanade in his flip flops, the sky above him something like the colour of a burst fountain pen on a white shirt.

In what seemed like the next moment I was being woken by my wife. She looked troubled. "I think my waters have broken," she told me. The wild beast we had been expecting, foam mouthed and full of claws, had finally knocked upon our door. My wife took hold of my hand with a squeeze. "You looked like you were having a bad dream. Come on, we need to go."

I got up from the sofa and grabbed the car keys, feeling fear and excitement already taking possession of my body. Everything in the next few hours, then days, became the fog of a dream that winds its way around reality. We became parents. It was as if this gift had been bestowed on us in exchange for the solidity of consciousness and sleep and the usual matters of day to day life. If we had been prepared it quickly began to feel like we were not prepared enough. We were parents to a baby boy – a warm, helpless gurgling battery that powered a kind of love utterly new in form and function. We were ecstatic and exhausted in equal measure.

It wasn't until a couple of weeks after the birth of Jack that I found myself alone at home. My wife was at her parents' with our baby. I spent the morning in something of a daze, not quite sure what to do with myself or my tiredness. Around lunch time my thoughts turned to John and I wondered how he had been in the last two weeks. I suddenly remembered that the phone box was being decommissioned and a feeling of panic rose up in me. I had to speak with him. Grabbing the telephone I went outside to the shady corner of the garden where there was a bench. I sat down and dialled the familiar number. I knew it was unlikely that John would just happen to be passing by the phone box but that wasn't important – in that moment it just felt good to be trying to speak with him. Perhaps it was my tiredness but I had a bad feeling that John was gone.

The telephone line clicked and hummed as if the wires themselves were considering the numerical combination I had keyed in.

"It is no longer possible to connect you. Please hang up and try again. It is no longer possible to connect you. Please hang up an…"

I did try again, and again. I felt sad and guilty that I had not called John earlier and I remembered how defeated he sounded the last time we had spoken. I felt bad for my oldest friend and as I sat in the shade, the phone still in my hand, my sadness for John became mixed up with fear for my son; I never wanted Jack to be alone, to be in anguish, to feel how cold the world can be even in the summer heat, and by letting John down I had in some way let down my child and the man he would become. The past, the present, the future, they all seemed to curl about each other. It all sounds so silly, I know, and I knew too that the anguish of life is unavoidable no matter what you do, but right then everything overwhelmed me and tears started to run down my cheeks.

I must have begun to drift into a sort of half sleep because I was pulled from my daze by the phone ringing in my hand.

"Hello?" I answered trying to sound normal.

"It's me!"

"John. I tried calling you. I'm so sorry." My brain was still muddled and I rubbed my face.

"Why you sorry? I'm guessing you've been a little busy recently."

"Yeah."

"So come on. Was it a boy or a girl?"

"A boy," I told him. "Jack."

"Congratulations man! That's great news. Is everyone doing ok?"

"Everyone is fine."

"You sure you're doing ok? You sound odd."

I laughed. "Where the hell are you John? I just called the phone box but it's disconnected."

"It's gone," he tells me. "Nothing but a stain on the pavement and a hole where cables used to be. I came and watched them take it away. I sat there with a bottle of wine and drank to it. Didn't take them more than an hour. I got so drunk and it was like I could see all these spirits of dead conversations being released into the air like balloons."

"I can't believe it's gone." I stood up and moved into the sunlight.

"All gone."

"So where are you?" I ask him. "You've found another telephone?"

"I don't know where I am," he said with a little laugh, "but everything is fine. I feel good."

"What do you mean you don't know where you are? Are you in Brightlea?"

"I don't think so. After the phone was torn down and I finished off the wine I felt pretty glum and out of it. I took a wander and went down to the beach and just kept walking. There were a lot of people around so I just kept walking and walking until everyone had disappeared."

I was staring at a bee trying to land successfully on the overgrown lavender, listening to what John was telling me. "When was this?" I ask.

"Don't know. It's hard to keep track. There are nights and there are days and one just becomes another. I was on the beach and there was no one else around and the sky, it was magnificent. Like blueberry slush."

"You're not making sense."

"Just listen to my story. I stripped down to my underpants and walked out into the sea. My god it was cold. But it felt good. It knocked the wine right out of me. It knocked everything out of me and I let it."

"Jesus," I said. "That's so dangerous."

"You're right, but I didn't care. I knew I would be ok. I just knew and then I saw something out in the water ahead of me. It was Stumpy! He was out there too just swimming and drifting. He was alive and young like when we worked at Crusoe's. He saw me and lifted his hand out of the water to wave at me with a big smile on his face. I tried to call to him but the noise of the water was just too loud and the swell kept making us disappear from each other's sight. I called but I don't know if he heard me."

My head started to feel cloudy again. "But none of that is possible," I told him. "It can't be real."

"I thought the same thing but I'm telling you I saw Stumpy. Suddenly I realised the sea was pulling me along the shore and I could not tell how far I had gone. When I looked back at the beach nothing was familiar, it was all sand dunes and sky. Eventually I started swimming and found myself back on the beach not far from my clothes."

"How long were you in the sea?"

"I couldn't tell. The sun had moved but that was all I knew. It didn't seem to matter. All I could think about was how refreshed I was. The sea had given me something."

"Yeah," I told him, "sickness and diarrhoea I should think."

"No," he said, brushing away my humour. "I had an idea for a story. A story that would really sing and make sense of everything, all those conversations from the telephone box. You put all those balloons together and it makes a giant picture."

"John," I said seriously. "Things have been a bit crazy with me the last couple of weeks and I know I'm frazzled but you're not making any sense. I'm worried for you."

"That's why I'm calling you," he said, excitement still in his voice. "I want to tell you that you shouldn't worry. I'm fine and I know what I'm doing now."

"But where are you?"

"In a phone box, maybe the last one on the planet. There are weeds growing in here and outside there's nothing, just an empty back road. My credit is going to run out so I need to tell you I've got to write this story. You've got a baby to think about so don't worry about me."

"I'll come and see you," I said. "Once things have settled down here."

"There's no need. I've got to go and it might be for a while but I'm doing just what I need to."

"But when will I hear from you again?"

"I don't know but I'm out here somewhere and that's all that matters."

I'm not certain if he had something more to say but the line began to beep and then I was listening to the dial tone. I think I must have been stood by the lavender with the phone in my hand for a few moments before I saw my wife, standing by the back door. Jack was in her arms looking like he'd just come round from some wondrous dream. He looked at me and gurgled happily.

My wife smiled. "Who were you talking to?" she asked.

FIDDLING ON THE BINK

I grew up at the seaside. I had a summer job for a few seasons as a donkey boy, giving rides to the holidaymakers on those sad looking creatures with names like Bess or Billy or Jake.

I walked for miles and miles across the sand, fifty yards down the beach and then turn around and fifty yards back, over and over again each day. My boss, whose name was Newman, owned the donkeys and had long since figured it all out. He cut the ends out of his plimsolls to let the sand escape as he trekked behind his animals. His toes were dark as creosote but his toenails were white as clouds.

When days were slow, Newman would say to me, "Nothing doing. Take a few donkeys and try fiddling on the bink." I would nod and do as he said.

The bink was a bulge of sand that had formed a short distance from the shore line. I'm not even certain if anyone else ever referred to it as 'the bink' but everyone who worked on the donkeys called it that. You had to be careful though. Newman's license did not allow him to take the donkeys on to that part of the beach. His patch was officially between the deckchair hire and the ice cream kiosk. Another donkey man he knew by the name of Benny got a fine for fiddling on the bink.

"Don't do a Benny," he would tell me when I set out for the felonious spot.

On a slow day the bink would often be worth the risk. Children always played down at the shore and if the tide had been and gone it would leave a small lagoon of water that drew the children and their parents alike. That was another reason you had to be careful; donkeys hate water and are liable to get jittery if you take them too close.

Newman wouldn't send just any donkey boy to the bink. He knew I could manage it and I always did. I worked for Newman for about three summers, in the sand and the sun and often the rain, but more often it was the sun on my skin and always the smell of the donkeys, always the idle tide lolling and industrious children roaring across wild space.

Maybe I used to moan too much then. Now that I am old I can only shake my head at my young self who grew tired of the sand. After the donkeys I got a job pumping petrol at a local garage because it paid five bob more. That was the job I did until I was about sixteen.

As a grown man I've had many jobs, mainly in factories. I have a lot of happy memories even though it was hard and often a joyless way to eke out my days. Now, when I think on it, it always seems that I never had it quite as good as when I walked the beach with the toes cut out of my shoes and occasionally fiddled on the bink.

CAPTAIN PARTY TIME

It's Captain Part Time! He's come with his magic broom to sweep the bad vibes from the carpet. Always check behind to see if Lieutenant Introspection is there too. Watch out for him – he's bad news. When you tell the Lieutenant to leave he says, "I'll come back when it's dark." Don't doubt that bastard and quickly bar the door. Sometimes the Captain can place a magic force field around it. I love that guy! Then it's just you and the Captain.

Waiting. For the sun to go down maybe. Waiting for the sun in the back garden to be at an angle so that the world lights up in a way that makes you feel right where you're supposed to be; the centre of the universe. Or at least your room, your street, your town, the landscape.

When you ask him where he's been, because it's been a while, he just shrugs and says, "At sea." You mirror his shrug and notice that he's wearing flip flops and his hat has a bright red feather in it. You like him even more.

So it's time to forget time. Time to step out on to the balcony and admire the view. Now the Captain is here that view is the same but different and anything is possible once more. It's like that old poker maxim, a chip and a chair. It's true. The Captain smiles. Your mind whirrs at the possible combinations of your thoughts, all the directions to explore. You are in perpetual anticipation of the now. It's the same feeling as wanting to dance: something just compels you to move. The Captain encourages you. He plugs in the oversized jet-age jukebox and its lights begin to glow. From within its mechanism there starts a hum.

LOW NOON

It was the morning a scarecrow ran across the field and got tangled up in the fence that I realised the game was really up.

I'd had the email of course, just like everybody else, but its information felt somehow remote and unreal. It all seemed too bureaucratic. No one could trace the source of it but it dropped into every inbox worldwide.

Online, many things were said in response to the announcement, as you would expect. They ranged from complete cynicism to outright panic. Things were debated everywhere of course, even in our little village of Low Scaraby people were talking and wondering.

Words to describe what was happening were scrambled for, with only one or two gaining currency in the popular imagination. Words such as *dissolving* and *dissolution* were favourites, though to me they sounded as if they were referring to a turd jammed in a sewer pipe. In time the chatter and the noise died away, as was predicted it might. Nothing very much happened for a while.

The scarecrow had been stuck since the early hours of the morning. Around seven it was light enough that I could investigate what had become snagged about the fence at the bottom of my garden. I was a little surprised to find a scarecrow well and truly caught by his arms and legs. I was even more surprised to hear the damn thing talk to me.

"Aren't you going to get me free?" it asked.

This seemed quite reasonable to me and the scarecrow had said it with such desperation that I obliged straightaway.

I never investigated too closely what he was stuffed with but his body was clothed in garments any farmer might have had. A navy coloured boiler suit was covered in a very dirty, very old donkey jacket. He wore a waistcoat cut from old plastic bags of Cooper's Cattle Feed. I decided to name him Cooper and he seemed quite happy with this.

Cooper's head was made from a piece of sacking on which sat a ragged woolly hat. I'm sorry to say that Cooper had no facial features, yet it did not stop me from making a connection with him. I knew when he was looking at me, I knew when he was thinking and I knew that he felt things just as I did. Whatever Cooper was, he needed help and I quickly ran to the cottage and returned with wire cutters to get him free. He managed to lift himself up and I took his arm around my shoulder. Together we made our way back up the garden. I did not think about it then, but it was perhaps the first time that Cooper had ever set foot inside a home.

I placed the strange creature in an armchair near the fire, but not too near, as he seemed to be cold and shivering. I sat across from him, not certain what to say or what to do. His plain, sack head appeared to look about my modest cottage, then turned to me with a sigh.

"Do you know what has happened? He asked in a quiet voice. "How it is that I am here? How it is that I am at all?"

I thought for a moment, listening to the crackle of the fire. I thought how pleasant this situation might be if things were normal. We could have been two friends enjoying nothing more than a chat by the fire on a cold winter's day. Yet things were not like that. Cooper was almost certainly not part of the normal order of things.

"I can only try and explain," I began, "and hope that it makes sense to you, though truth be told, I don't think it makes sense to anyone really. Before I begin, may I ask you a question?"

"Of course, yes. A question." Cooper seemed quite intrigued by the notion. "I don't believe I have ever answered a question before."

"That's just it," I told him. "Can you tell me anything about 'before'? I mean, when did you become what I see in front of me now? When did you begin to think and move?"

"That is an excellent question," he said thoughtfully and I couldn't help but like him more. "I cannot tell you anything of before," Cooper went on. "All I know is that I became aware of myself and the field in which I stood, sometime earlier. It was still dark and I felt frightened and alone. I managed to get free of the pole where I was stuck. Once I realised I was able to move my legs and arms that was it; I started running and running. I think I might have crossed two fields before I managed to get myself caught in your fence. Then you rescued me and now here I am. Do you have any idea what is going on?"

His blank face looked at me and although it was expressionless I could tell that Cooper was troubled, just as everybody had become troubled.

"I have some idea of what is occurring," I said. "As much as anyone does. You see, the entire world has been informed of something so terrible that up until recently no one knew if it were real or not. Yet, I think now, people are beginning to grasp the absolute horror of it all."

"What is this horror?" he asked looking down at himself and pinching his own arm. "After what has happened to me, I think it is something which I might understand. I mean, waking up in the way that I have is very exciting, but it is also very frightening."

"People are calling it the dissolution," I told him. "The slow cancellation of everything."

Cooper sat back in my armchair, his empty face looking at me.

I tried to explain things as far as I understood them. I told him, as simply as I could, about the worldwide message that everyone had received. I told him how the media had dispersed the information globally and how it had created doubt, anger, fear and confusion in equal measure.

"But who was the original message from?" he asked.

"That's just it," I told him. "In the end no one could be sure. Lots of experts claimed one thing or another. Some said it was alien intelligence determined to wipe us out. Some said it was humanity of the future wanting to destroy us because of what the future must hold. Others said it was proof that the world is nothing but a simulation created by a vast intelligence we cannot begin to fathom. No one knew for certain. In the end a lot of people decided it was a hoax and just got on with their lives."

Cooper pushed his woolly hat back and scratched his head. "Wow," he said. "How do I fit in to all of this?"

He couldn't read but he could understand pictures. I showed him a newspaper that was three days old. I turned to the pages where there were photos of statues walking down a street in Italy. Ancient bits of marble had come to life and decided to take a stroll. I flicked further on and showed him the pictures where an entire piece of the Alaskan wilderness had disappeared. Not destroyed. Disappeared and become a white blank space of nothing. Scientists believed about ten thousand acres in all had vanished and it wasn't only in Alaska. Similar reports were coming from all over the world, even a town in Bulgaria had allegedly disappeared overnight.

Cooper nodded. "So I am just a part of this?" He looked at me and I believe he saw a weariness in my eyes. "Strange happenings," he added.

"Yes," I said, wanting a drink. "The slow cancellation of everything."

"I'll pour you something strong," Cooper said as if reading my mind. He got up and moved to my drinks cabinet where half a bottle of scotch sat. "Can anything be done?" he asked.

"I don't think so," I shrugged. "I think your appearance might indicate that the dissolution is gathering pace, at least in this neck of the woods."

"I'm sorry," he said.

"We could try and outrun it. We could leave this place but the same things are happening all over," I told him. "We might just go in the wrong direction and find ourselves somewhere that is suddenly snuffed out."

We both continued to sit by the fire, watching its flames scramble up the flue like a troop of fox cubs leaving their den.

"Did you have a plan?" Cooper asked me after a while.

"No," I told him, gazing into my drink. "I thought I would just wait and see."

"Wait and see." The scarecrow repeated the phrase. "I suppose that your waiting and seeing was a stroke of luck for me, otherwise I'd still be tangled up in that fence not knowing what was going on." He looked about him again. "Is there no one else here?" he asked. "Have you no companion?"

"My wife died," I told him, turning to the foxes in the fire once more. "It was a while ago. She got ill and died and so I suppose the dissolution of everything sort of suited me." I looked at Cooper, his blank face staring at me.

"Dying," he said slowly. "That's the opposite of what has happened to me, isn't it. I have undied, haven't I?"

"I'm not sure," I said. "Very little seems to make sense these days. But you are certainly alive now."

The day continued. I left Cooper with the newspaper. He seemed happy enough looking at the pictures of all the strange events that were going on across the world. I tried to get on with my usual morning routine; I brought in firewood from the shed, I did the other chores that I always liked to do. My routine had been the same when my wife was still alive and hadn't changed in the years since her passing. She always liked that I kept myself busy and not under her feet. At mid-morning I stopped and checked on Cooper. I had given him all the old newspapers I had and he had been flicking through them, still trying to make sense of everything.

"All so strange," he told me, looking up from a week old copy of The Times.

I decided to check on the latest events and turned on the television, or at least tried to turn it on. Every channel was a blank screen.

"This looks sinister," I said.

Cooper nodded blankly.

I turned on the radio. It was an old Decca radiogram that had been a wedding gift from my uncle. There was news of an increase in the dissolution of reality across the UK. The Houses of Parliament had vanished only to return nearly three hundred miles away, falling from the sky and raining down in tiny fragments across the north, from Newcastle to Carlisle, some pieces no bigger than a golf ball, while other bits of masonry were as big as cars. Panic and confusion was breaking out everywhere.

"I think you should see this," Cooper said. He had moved to the window and was looking out along the garden. The fence he had gotten caught in was no longer there. In its place there was nothing. Complete whiteness, like a blanket of thick fog had drifted across the fields and stopped at the boundary of my cottage. The miasma extended well beyond my garden in a great white wall, as if a blind had been pulled down across the farmland. I went to the front window and looked out. From that side everything was normal; the fields and the lane that ran into Low Scaraby, still there, just as they had always been.

"We seem to be right on the edge of it," I told Cooper. He was still gazing at the vast whiteness that was hovering by the cherry tree I had planted for my wife on her fiftieth birthday.

"Do you think it will swallow us?" Cooper asked. There was more wonder in his voice than dread and I felt sorry that the thing which had bestowed him life would soon likely swallow him and take back what it had given

"Let's have another drink," I said.

We sat ourselves again by the warmth of the fire. I drank while he cradled an empty glass in a gesture of solidarity. "It tastes very fine," he joked, pretending to drink. Every once in a while one of us would get up and take another look out the window. For a long time there was no change, but then as dusk fell the cherry tree had disappeared into the nothing.

"We could leave," Cooper suggested. "We could make our way toward the village and then decide what to do from there."

"I'm staying," I told him. "The village might have already disappeared. Besides, I'm happy here."

Cooper nodded thoughtfully. "You don't mind if I stay here, do you?"

"I think it would be best if you did," I said looking toward the window.

"That way neither of us will be alone," Cooper concluded.

After a short time it had grown dark. I couldn't stand to sit and do nothing and I think the whiskey had begun to embolden me, or at least loosen my sense of dread. "Come on," I said to Cooper, "let's go outside and take a look."

In my garden the moonlight was like I had never seen it before, nor I suppose, like Cooper had ever seen it. There was a near full moon shining in one half of a cloudless dark. The other portion of the sky was lost to the great blanket of white nothingness that had paused halfway along my garden. The moonlight shimmered on the fog bank, giving the night an iridescence like it was made of silver tissue.

"It's drifting closer, isn't it?" Cooper said, gazing up at the wall of white. "What do you think it's like inside of it?"

It was a question that had not occurred to me, or probably to anyone else. The world had been more concerned with being extinguished and how to prevent it, than to wonder what might have been on the other side of the dissolution.

"I suppose it isn't like anything," I shrugged. "It's hard to think of."

"So maybe there is something," Cooper went on. "I mean it is possible, isn't it? If statues can walk and scarecrows come to life, then it's possible there is something inside of it. Why not?"

I looked again at the thing that hovered in my garden; nothing more than a cloud, it shimmered from the blades of grass at my feet, up to the blackness of the night sky far above. I could have believed that the dissolution was staring back at me, waiting and thinking.

"You want to step inside it, don't you?" I asked Cooper. He was transfixed like me.

"Why not?" he replied. "If it's going to swallow everything up anyway." He turned to me. "This has been the most curious day of my life. I could end it just as it began; stepping into the unknown."

"I think that is a good idea," I told him.

"One of my best," he said with a chuckle.

Nothing more needed to be said. I gazed behind to have a final look at my little cottage, the home I had made with my wife, the place I had been living quietly and alone. Then I turned to face the cloud and Cooper was at my side. We looked at one another and nodded. Instinctively we both took a half step back and together we launched ourselves into

THANKS

Immense thanks to Melody Clark and Tom Wickstead for being a part of the madness and the team. Of course I am ever grateful to my family and my friends for the love and support that is always there.

Thanks to the village of Low Scaraby for allowing me to walk among its stories and its people.

About the author:

Richard Daniels is the author of *Our Bright Dark Summer*

He began writing on the back of bus tickets and sick bags and formed a writers group which only met in graveyards at midnight. His thoughts are frequently monitored by intelligences from other dimensions. Usually on Tuesdays.

Instagram: @the_writer_richard_daniels

We are an independent publisher of poetry and fiction run by a Plastic Brain. Our aim is to find the literary underground and smear it into your mind hole. The Plastic Brain would like to meld minds with you – this is nothing to fear.

Find us on social media and listen to our podcast, Crash Course in Brain Surgery. The Plastic Brain is here for your cerebral needs with books and more.

Also available from Plastic Brain Press:

Sending A Drunk Text Whilst Sober

by Simon Widdop

Go to:

plasticbrainpress.com

26934261R00193

Made in the USA
Columbia, SC
21 September 2018